SLEEPOVERS

ADVANCED PRAISE FOR *SLEEPOVERS*

"This collection stands out in the field of current Southern fiction."
—*PUBLISHERS WEEKLY,* **STARRED REVIEW**

"A deeply human, unforgettable debut."   —*BOOKLIST*

"*Sleepovers* is an unflinching collection through which the complexities, curiosities, and complications of rural Southern life come through."
—*FOREWORD REVIEWS*

"I see in this collection a steely writer, one deeply moved by her place and her people, but also fully committed to the truth no matter how dark or difficult or complicated it may be."
—LAUREN GROFF, CONTEST JUDGE AUTHOR OF *FLORIDA*

"There's some kind of crazy magic at work here—the way that Ashleigh Bryant Phillips takes all the little pieces of daily life that are there in plain sight just laying around and when she gathers them together they become holy, hilarious, transcendent, and unspeakably beautiful. Phillips is shockingly talented."   **—MESHA MAREN, AUTHOR OF** *SUGAR RUN*

"With *Sleepovers*, Phillips has intimately given us an entirely new way of seeing traditional life in small-town America. This book is so hard-core, so hard-won, so much a fabric of complicated gorgeous beauty. This is a book unlike any other written before it."
—REBECCA LEE, AUTHOR OF *BOBCAT AND OTHER STORIES*

"I can't remember a time when I've read a story collection so funny and sad and lyrical, all at the same time. In *Sleepovers*, Ashleigh Bryant Phillips gives us a book that's so much more than a story collection. This book is haunted."   **—SCOTT MCCLANAHAN, AUTHOR OF** *THE SARAH BOOK*

"Every once in awhile, a book comes along and slugs you upside the head, making you wonder why you've been wasting your time with those other comparably bland and polite books. *Sleepovers* is that book, that slugger. Ashleigh Bryant Phillips is a dazzling and mighty talent."
—JULIET ESCORIA, AUTHOR OF *JULIET THE MANIAC*

"Like me, I'm sure you will also feel like you're sitting on a porch listening to these stories, knowing they're being told to you out of necessity from an urgent and generous place." —STEVEN DUNN, AUTHOR OF *WATER & POWER*

"Ashleigh Bryant Phillips' voice helps readers understand that being nurtured and wounded by the South can cause various times, and places, and norms to be mixed up together." —CLYDE EDGERTON, AUTHOR OF *RANEY*

"The people in these stories are unflinching, and undeniably, uncomfortably real. We know these folks from the post office, the grocery store, from church. This book is otherworldly beautiful." —WENDY BRENNER, AUTHOR OF *PHONE CALLS FROM THE DEAD*

Sleepovers

Ashleigh Bryant Phillips

HUB CITY PRESS
SPARTANBURG, SC

Copyright © 2020
Ashleigh Bryant Phillips

Book Design: Meg Reid
Cover art: "Diptych 1" © George Wylesol
Copyeditors: Kalee Lineberger
Printed in Saline, MI by McNaughton & Gunn

Library of Congress Cataloging-in-Publication Data

Phillips, Ashleigh Bryant, author.
Sleepovers / Ashleigh Bryant Phillips.
Spartanburg, SC : Hub City Press, [2020]
LCCN 2019057792 (print) | ISBN 9781938235665 (paperback)
LCC PS3616.H4524 A6 2020 (print) | DDC 813/.6—dc23
LC record available at https://lccn.loc.gov/2019057792

Lines from "40th Chorus" by Jack Kerouac published in *San Francisco Blues*.
Lines from "Love Song: First Version, 1915" by William Carlos Williams
published in *The Collected Poems of William Carlos Williams Volume 1*.

HUB CITY
PRESS

186 West Main St.
Spartanburg, SC 29306
1.864.577.9349
www.hubcity.org
www.twitter.com/hubcitypress

For everyone back home, especially

B.B.P.

S.B.P.

N.B.A.

D.L.B.

W.E.B.

D.C.B.

And the ones in the stars

S.G.

M.R.L.

L.B.G.

A.B.B.

E.W.B.

J.E.B.

J.A.B.

D.L.P.

Contents

"We do not like to be told that we are in a trap, and that there is nothing we can do to get out; still less do we like to realize it as a vivid experience. But there is no other way of release."

Alan Watts

Shania

On the day we met, she told me she was named after the sexiest country music star alive. And that she knew how to fire a gun. And that she was one hundred percent Cherokee.

My mama says I'm named after nobody. We don't have a gun in our house. I have blonde hair and blue eyes.

I'm so jealous of her that I talk about it with Jesus when I say my prayers at night. It's May and I'm gonna turn eight on July 30th. She's just turned seven and is about two heads shorter than me.

When I went to her house for the first time, her daddy had just started fixing up the balcony. She lives in the big gray house on Main Street. Mama says it's Victorian. It's the only Victorian on Main Street that has the balcony falling apart. Pieces of the fancy white trim round the roof is missing. They're all in the yard. You can see 'em from the road.

There's a history book of the town at the town hall. And one time when Mama went up there to pay the water bill, I found a picture of that house in that history book. It said her house was built when the town was "booming." The picture was black and white but under the picture it said the house used to be painted robin's egg blue.

I don't tell her about that picture. But I think about it when I go into her house. There's no blinds or curtains on the windows. They got sheets hung up instead, like old sheets. Probably her baby sheets from her baby bed.

And there's this one big window in the living room and it don't have a sheet. And her grandmamma sits there a lot in her chair. And the sunlight comes in on her face and it makes all the dust in there shine and float around her like magic. And when her grandmamma breathes real heavy, you can see how the sparkles dance around her. And when she sleeps, sometimes I get as close to her as I can to see how deep the wrinkles go in her face. And one time when I was real close to her like that I asked her grandmamma about animal spirits. If my kitten carried inside it the heart of a big old ghost. See she told me that her grandmamma talks in her sleep. But she didn't tell me anything. She never says much to me at all. Her grandmamma has real fat arms.

Her mama has a big butt and says "he's hot" when some man comes on the TV. Her daddy has a mustache and kills all kinds of animals, hunts them all the time. One time he killed a deer and her mama cooked it. She sneaked into the fridge to show me, because she's not allowed to go in the fridge or her daddy yells and the yelling makes me want to get into the back of the closet like we had to do that one time. But when she put the deer meat in my hand she told me to not think about Bambi, just hush and eat it. I thought it tasted a little like roast beef, but it was dry.

She likes to show off her mama and daddy's waterbed. Seems like every time I go over there, the first thing we do is go into their bedroom and she pokes the water bed to make it slosh. I told Mama about it and she said that waterbeds are bad for your back. But there's one huge picture on the wall in their bedroom, right above the bed. It's an Indian warrior sitting on a horse with spots on him. They are in the desert somewhere. And there's not any cactuses or trees, but there's a mountain way back behind them. And it's about to be night time because the sky is purple. The horse's head is down. And the Indian has white and red paint on his chest. It looks messy, maybe he's sweaty. His leg muscles are big and looks like he's squeezing the horse with them as hard as he can. And he's sitting slumped over, with his hair in his face. There's an arrow sticking out of his back.

She always sees me looking at that picture every time we go in there. But she never says anything about that Indian. I guess it ain't no big deal to her. She don't go to pow wows. She don't go to church either. And the Baptist church is right there beside her house.

One time I was there close to supper and we were swinging on her swing set and the church bells started ringing a church song. We had a bunch of her beaded bracelets on and they was making lots of noise when we swang up and down. I told her we were making music. All we needed was a big ol' drum to beat on like Hi-a-wa-tha. Jun-a-lus-ka. Pow-ha-tan. She thought that was funny. Her backyard has roly polies, no grass, and a big mean dog tied up at the edge of it. She hates to feed that dog. His name is Butchie. I watch her feed him. And one day that dog jumped on her and knocked her down. She got up and came to me with her elbow bleeding. She told me she had fell on a busted bottle. The blood was coming out quick but she didn't cry. Their backyard has dog food cans and cigarettes and broken bottles all over it. I found a piece of glass and pulled it down my hand like people in the movies. And the blood came out and I didn't cry either and I held her elbow. Our blood mixed together. And we found a clean spot in the dirt where it was cool and we sat there long enough for us to be blood sisters.

I did a rain dance in the front yard like she showed me how to do. I put my hands to the sky just like her. And I danced so much! Grass got stuck in my toes! And the bottom of my feet turned green! But I got mad cause I couldn't get it to rain. Mama says the corn needs rain real bad now.

Everyday morning I check my hairbrush for a brown hair like hers. And today I found one. It's proof of my native blood. I put it in an envelope to the father thunder god. I think he's an eagle with spreaded out wings and turquoise eyes. I write a letter to him, but at the end I remember I don't know his address. And I know that she knows it. And I bet if she don't know, her grandmamma knows. So I need to go ask them about it.

I ask Mama if I can go to her house after dinner, but she says that I can't go over to her house no more. She says that her daddy hit her mama till she was 'bout dead last night. So I'm gonna go and try to slip her some secret notes. I can get some tape from the kitchen drawer, walk up to her house at night and tape it to the seat of her swing. I think that'll be a good place for her to find them. I want to tell her it's gonna be okay. And we'll keep telling each other things like that. But what happens is I never end up leaving her any notes. We go to different schools. Her daddy leaves them, stops fixing up the balcony. More and more of it falls in the yard. By the time I go to college the yard's all soggy, shit white.

And last time I was home, Mama sent me uptown for an onion. And I saw her working there in J.J.'s. She was real pregnant, shoulda been off her feet. I went to her checkout line and all she said was "Hello" like you're supposed to do. And when she opened the cash register, the drawer bumped her big baby belly. And while she counted my change, I thought about her in that house, floating alone in the middle of that waterbed, tracing shapes on her belly. And when she handed me the change, her fingernails grazed my palm.

Charlie Elliott

You don't know if you were born wrong or if it's because on the way home from the hospital there was a big storm and your daddy wrecked the car and your mama dropped you in the floorboard. Y'all all survive but you aren't right. You are the oldest son. You grow up to be the tallest of your brothers and sisters.

You learn everything late. Start walking when you're four. Your legs look like toothpicks. You aren't able to help on the farm. But you know how big it feels, especially when you look at it from your upstairs bedroom window. It stretches back far behind the house and you watch the tops of your daddy and brothers and sisters heads in the rows suckering tobacco. You can always tell which one is which. You sit at home with your mama and watch her iron and play the piano. You are decent at shucking corn but feel you could be better if you didn't shake so bad. Your daddy doesn't understand. He thinks you can control it. He yells at you and tells you to control it. You sit angry.

When you get nervous it's hard to keep your hands steady. Since you're the oldest your mama wants you to sit next to your daddy at the table but sometimes you spill the peas from your spoon so your daddy makes you wear a bib and sit far away from him. It's hard for you to write and you never learn cursive because of it. You don't finish school because you don't see the need to. You don't drive the tractor. You don't learn to drive a car. Your mama wants you to always stay where she can see you.

You have to wear glasses. You can't play sports. When your younger brothers are playing their basketball and baseball and football games you think about them having a good time and scoring for the home team and getting high-fives. So you wait for them on the front porch thinking about this and you want to hit them real hard right in the face. When they come home sometimes you hurt them so bad that your mama calls the doctor in town to come out to the house. The doctor tells you you don't know how strong you are and while your brothers are saying you're crazy, while they're covering their faces in the corner and blood's running from their mouths, while your sisters are hiding in the closet, your mama begs the doctor not to say nothing to people in town. The doctor promises he'll never say a word every time he gives you a shot to knock you out.

You go into town with your family to the bank and feel that everyone there knows how you are and you feel them looking at you and your stick-stiff legs and shaky head. You want to leave them all, leave everything and go somewhere.

At the family reunion when you're seventeen, you want to bury all your daddy's new baby chicks in the soft dirt in the path next to the old family homeplace. You want to bury them in that soft dirt with their heads sticking out. And you want to call all your family outside and you want them to stand on the porch while you lawnmower all the baby chicks heads off— in a nice little row. You want all of your kin to see you do something real terrible like that and then you want to run and cut across the fields and the swamp until you can catch a train and go far, far away. You think about this plan over and over. And then you get too scared in the chicken coop trying to get the bitties because the mama hens peck at your hands so bad you can't stand it. You know that means you're sensitive. You're a wuss. And for the rest of the afternoon you sit alone under a gum tree looking at your pecked hands, while your brothers and sisters and cousins race around and around you. You stay there in the middle of it all and watch everything and don't talk to anyone until you decide to go and wash your hands in the sink. And when you come up you see your head is still shaking in the mirror. And your glasses are filthy too.

Your mama prays with you every night. Prays with you longer than she does with your brothers or sisters. You think it's because she's afraid of you. She tells you to listen for God's still, quiet voice.

Your daddy tells you that no woman will ever love you. You believe him. All your younger brothers are away at war repairing bombers on Air Force bases. Their girlfriends with curled hair come up on the porch on late Saturday afternoons and ask if y'all have heard any news lately. You sit on the bottom step and stretch out your big toe and try to make circles with it in the dirt, but they come out rectangles. You hear how sad these girls are asking. And you wonder if your brothers will ever know how sad they sound.

And your mama listens to the radio at night. You hear a story on there about a door-to-door salesman who becomes the hero of the town by keeping the citizens from brawling each other at a town meeting. He's a friend to everyone and when he stands up at the meeting everyone looks up to him. They think he's so great that they want to make him mayor but he humbly declines. You decide then you want to be a door-to-door salesman.

Your mama says no, she does not want you leaving the house with strangers like they are. But you know she really means she does not want you leaving the house with YOU like you are. You tell your daddy it's what you want to do and he says it ain't right either. Your baby sisters believe you the most and help you shine your shoes and clean your glasses.

You order pens and pencils and office supplies with money you've been stealing from the offering plate all these years to get out of this place. You put on your nice clean button-up your mama ironed. You buy a cheap briefcase from the dime store and know that you're the first person in your family to have a briefcase. You ask your daddy to drop you off in town and he doesn't say a word the whole ride. And you go door to door starting on Main Street and then working your way back into the neighborhoods; all the streets are named after trees in town. People open their doors because they know who you are, or they've heard of you. They don't seem to be afraid of you cleaned up with a briefcase.

A nice lady opens the door on Peachtree Street and she's got one of those faces that feels familiar like you've known her all your life. She buys a bunch of colored paper for her daughter who likes to draw. You ask how old her daughter is and she is four years younger than you. You ask what school she went to and she says that she kept her at home. You see her daughter peek at you from the hall and you think that maybe she was born wrong too. You figure she has never left this house. And you want to get her out of it.

The next week you ask the woman if you can visit with her daughter. She brings you down the hall and into the sun room where her daughter is drawing. She's quiet for a while and then she looks up and tells you she likes to sit in here and watch the birds outside. The light falls in on her hair like beach sunshine in the movies. There's plants growing all around her. It's like a jungle and you sit in the wicker chair across from her and wait for her to talk to you, like she's a magical animal behind all the vines and leaves. All you can figure is that she's just very, very shy. You think maybe you would have been this way too if you didn't grow up in such a loud family.

Her mother takes you two to the movies to see *South Pacific* and everything is going really nice until you get to the part when they're jumping in the waterfall and swimming and you wish you could jump in the water. You think of your brothers and sisters swimming in the creek on the farm, laughing and swimming. You wish you could swim. How the cool water would feel like, moving so freely in it. You feel yourself getting upset, the popcorn starts to tremble in your hands and you're afraid you're going to spill it. But then the girl holds her hand out in front of you, like she's asking you to hold it. You hold her hand, she calms you.

You start saving money really hard. You start working really hard. Start selling paper and pens all over. You start thumbing rides to Virginia. People in Conway who pass you say that you can get to Norfolk quicker than they can just driving. It's this myth that starts about you. And people still talk about it to this day.

Everyone in town knows you by now, they say, "Hey! It's Charlie!" when you walk into the bank or the grocery or the café. They all know you and they've all talked to you and you feel important.

You get written up in the paper. The paper says real good things. You look like a real professional in the picture with your briefcase and nice hat on. You're standing beside the road, squinting at the camera. It says: *Here Comes Charlie! April, 1960.*

The next time you see the girl on Peachtree Street you show her the article. And she giggles and says that she's already seen it. That she's cut it out and hung it up in her room above her desk. You dream of her room and what she has on her desk. Colored paper and charcoal and colored pens and watercolors, nothing too harsh, only graceful colors. She goes to her room and comes back with drawings of birds.

You haven't told anyone this but you feel like you need to tell her about what you wanted to do to those baby chicks that time at the family reunion. And she listens without being afraid. She says it's okay, we all get angry sometimes, we all want to run away sometimes.

She points to the bird feeder outside the sunroom window where she sees her birds. Y'all wait and watch a bluebird come to the feeder. You're afraid of hurting others but you feel it in your heart you can never hurt her. You know this more than anything. Before the bluebird flies away you ask her to marry you and she says yes.

Your daddy says that no two people like the two of you should be together in marriage. You tell him you have your own money and punch him in the face in front of your mama. When your daddy falls back, the look on his face is both surprised and proud. He does not hit you back.

Your mama plays the piano at your wedding and your sisters make cakes. It's so hot in the church that June that your new wife swears she saw sweat roll off your nose. She'll always love to remind you of this, and you'll deny it every time just to see her laugh. Your mama and sisters help your new wife hang up her bird drawings in the house. They put them in the places that look the best. Your new wife insists that the bluebird must be hung over the bed.

You feel it above you when you kiss her in bed. Your bedroom becomes a far, far away jungle. It feels like strange and beautiful branches lean heavy and circle from the ceiling, from the sky. You're happy when she takes off her nightgown by herself. You're surprised when she takes your hands and puts them on her body. When she pulls you to her by your belt. When she's under you she's soft and warm. You hold her without shaking.

The first time you come inside her, she kisses you all around your face like a rainbow. You think of her watercolors. You think of God. Maybe it's His still, quiet voice you're hearing when she sounds out pleasure.

You start to read the Bible she gave you when y'all got married. You like Colossians 3:12-14.

Put on therefore, as the elect of God, holy and beloved, bowels of mercies, kindness, humbleness of mind, meekness, longsuffering; Forbearing one another, and forgiving one another, if any man have a quarrel against any: even as Christ forgave you, so also do ye. And above all these things put on charity, which is the bond of perfectness.

You write it on a piece of paper and put it on the refrigerator. Your wife helps you pray about all the anger you've always had. You start tithing at church. You get baptized. You put on a compassionate heart. And send your mama and brothers and sisters letters apologizing for whatever hurt you caused them.

Your mama passes away from cancer right before Christmas the year y'all got married. And in front of all her unopened presents your daddy looks at you and your wife with her hand on your knee like y'all are dumb. Turns his back to y'all to face the rest of the family. Your brothers and sisters drink whiskey and play cards and laugh loudly. Your wife does not say much to them and she follows you to the kitchen every time you get up to make her more chocolate milk. Your sisters tell her they like her sweater. Your nieces and nephews ask her to draw them giraffes.

She cries to you when you get home because she can only draw birds. You comfort her. You protect her. You tell her that you love her for who she is.

You tell her that riding with your sisters to Belk's the next afternoon would be good for her. She never gets out of the house. It'll be good for her to get out. You give her some money to buy her a pretty new dress.

While she's out you think of what kind of dress she's gonna get. How she'll look coming home into the door. If she'll spin with her new dress on. You're thinking of this as you sit down for lunch at your dining room table. You look out the dining room window and wonder how your wife's cactuses are blooming in the winter weather. The blooms are so many, hanging heavy, bursting bright pink. Stars falling together all at once. You think she has made you a better person for being able to notice things like that. You tell yourself not to forget to ask her about the blooms. You die there choking on a peanut butter sandwich.

When your wife comes home she is wearing exactly the pretty new dress you wanted her to get. It's lilac with small white polka dots and it flows down her like waves. She puts your head in her lap and sits next to you at the table. She traces your ear with the silk hem of her dress until they take you away.

At your funeral the church is packed. People are standing up at the back, people are all in the balcony, people are sitting back in the Sunday school rooms. People from all over North Carolina and Virginia.

Outside the church your daddy tells the funeral director that your wife will sit behind your family. The funeral director says, But she's Mr. Charlie's wife. And your daddy says I'm paying for it so you're gonna do what I want.

At the graveside after it's all over, the mayor finds your wife crying in the crowd, she's between your baby sisters. The mayor gives her a key to the town in a cedar box. He says it's in your honor. He says you're a hero. The plaque on the box says your name.

Over the next couple of months your sisters come and visit your wife. Try to comfort her. But she only wants to read the Bible in a rocking chair. She takes down the bluebird above y'alls bed and places it in the back of the closet behind your briefcase. She only sleeps on the couch. Her younger brother moves in and lives with her until she dies of old age.

When she dies your daddy is still alive. He's in a wheelchair and chews on cigars but he does not want your wife buried next to you. He makes sure it doesn't happen. Everyone in town is upset by it. So when your daddy finally dies at 102, your brothers and sisters raise enough money to move her next to you in the family plot. The brother you used to beat up the most brings flowers for you and your wife when he's in town. He thinks about you every day, he dreams of you whistling as you walk with your briefcase. You never whistled though, you hummed. Yes, you always hummed.

Mind Craft

I was masturbating when Cole knocked on my door and told me Queenie had bit him.

"I ain't gonna die," he said. "She's bit me a bunch of times."

He held out his arm and stood real still and I touched it gentle with my masturbating smell fingers. His skin was raised around two little punctures and it was bleeding, right where her fangs went in. I've never seen a snake bite before. He said his mama puts apple cider vinegar and baking soda on it to take out the soreness. Cole's a scrappy boy. I believed him.

I coulda called Rhonda but seeing as she's the one who called me down here to look after Cole and Daddy while she was gone, I figured I shouldn't. She's a saint for my daddy. And she'd been wanting to go on that ladies motorcycle trip to Dollywood for a long time. She'd been sending me pictures of them riding the rides all morning. I didn't want to ruin her trip.

I got the baking soda and apple cider vinegar out the kitchen cabinet for Cole and watched him make it into a paste. Daddy was out in his tool shed drinking Crown and Mountain Dew from his special shrimp cup with the little pink shrimp shaking his booty on it. I knew he was upset about Cole's bite, worried what Rhonda would do when she found out. But I'd never seen him like this. Rhonda said he's been much more emotional since she's been getting him to ween off the weed.

While me and Cole waited for the paste to sit on his bite a little, I figured since it was on my mind I might as well ask him. "Just between you and me," I said, "how often do you see Daddy Bill this bent out of frame?"

"Oh, I don't know, like a lot." Cole spun around on the top of his stool. "Mama told me he's had a sad life, said that he raised you all by himself." Then he stopped himself spinning. "Did your mama really leave y'all to be with another lady?"

I told him yeah.

Then he asked me when was the last time I saw her.

And I said I didn't remember.

Then he asked me if I ever talked to her on the phone. And I said, "No."

"Not even for your birthday?"

"No," I said.

"Don't you miss her," he said.

I shook my head no and bit down on my fingers and tasted

my smell. I was washing my hands at the sink when I heard Cole behind me.

"Don't you want to know where she is?"

I just got out my phone and pulled up what to do about a python bite. "Look," I told him, "this says we need to wash it now. And get some Neosporin."

"We need to ride to Walmart for that," he said. "I used it all on my knee last week." He pointed to his scabby little knee.

When we told Daddy we were going to Walmart, he perked up the way he would around me when I was little. "Now look here, I know what's going on," he said. He put his arm around Cole, "This boy here's been wanting to go to the Walmart all damn month. His mama don't go to the Walmart for nothing. She don't believe in it." Then he looked at me, "I don't know why but she don't believe in the Walmart, Maddy." Then he pulled Cole closer to him, "Now tell what it is you want at the Walmart, son. Go on now and tell us."

"*Minecraft*," Cole said, smiling.

I started laughing.

"This boy wants that Mind Craft, that video game," Daddy laughed too and finished off his Crown and Mountain Dew.

I'd heard of *Minecraft*. It's what Patrick plays all the time. When I get done with classes and go to his place I can hear the music coming from the living room as soon as I come in the door. And there he is, sitting there in a trance shooting arrows into zombies. And I sit next to him hoping he'll put his arm around me or something. Because he's always got night shifts delivering pizzas. But nothing. Then when he does touch me he is full on boner and ready to go and so we go to his bedroom and we have sex and then he comes and we lay there a little and he lets me lay on his chest and I listen to his heartbeat and he tells me that I need to talk about my mama more. Patrick says my mama has shaped me into who I am now. He says she is still shaping me. He says this because, among other things, I take the pillow cases off pillows when I sleep. He's a philosophy major. And I already know what Daddy would say about him if they met. He'd say his handshake felt limp as a dishrag.

But I think it's pretty good sex. My dormmates tell me about guys going down on them like it's really wonderful like they're in another world. Patrick has only done it to me twice since we've been together and I don't think I ever came when he was down there. I mean, I didn't feel any different. I think it's 'cause I don't shave down there. When we first started dating Patrick said that some girls shaved the whole thing and he asked me if I ever did that and I said no. So one day I did it to surprise him and it took forever and then he didn't even like it that much, I don't think, and I hated how it made me itchy and I looked like a baby. I looked his ex up on Facebook and she was sitting on a yacht in a bikini, with a big bow in her hair. Patrick said her daddy was real rich. Christine was her name. They lived together and everything.

At Walmart, Daddy gave Cole a piggyback ride to look at some tools and I grabbed the Neosporin and went to get some hamburger for supper. Hamburger Helper is what me and Daddy always made together when I was growing up. He'd smoke a fat joint and add a lot of extra cheese. Rhonda don't like it too much because it ain't that healthy. When she moved in she planted a garden. It's off the porch he finally finished with her help. She's always sending me back to school with fresh tomatoes, enough for the whole hall. But I wanted that night to be like old times. So I got the meat that looked the best and headed on to the electronics and games.

When Daddy and Cole won't there, I figured they were still looking around. Daddy loves to look at everything in Walmart. Him and Cole were probably caught up in some rods and reels.

The girl who was working in electronics and games had huge breasts. I'd never seen her before. And I thought what I always think when I see huge breasts. I wondered what it would be like to suck on them. They would probably be nice and soft in my mouth. Patrick would say this has something to do with breast-feeding and my mama. I don't know if she breastfed me or not.

Her nametag said "Cammie". I asked her if they had Mind Craft for Xbox 360.

"You mean *Minecraft*?"

"Oh yeah, sorry," I laughed. "My daddy calls it Mind Craft."

"Well, yeah we have it, people have been going nuts over it lately." She led me to the shelf where it was and grabbed it for me. "You ever play it," she asked.

I looked down at her handing it to me and said, "No, but my boyfriend does."

"It looks boring. I mean everything is just blocks." She looked at the block-headed people between my thumbs. "Is it boring?"

I didn't know what to say to that. I was thinking about how big her nipples might be compared to mine and I said, "The music is kind of relaxing."

"Oh," she said. "Well I'll ring you up now I guess."

I told her I didn't want the receipt. I told her that when a half-drunk man and a kid with a swollen arm came up to buy *Minecraft* to tell them that Maddy had already bought it for them and she was waiting in the truck.

"Okay," she said. It sounded like she said it in a way she doesn't say it every day.

Patrick called me on the way to the truck. He's always worried when I'm at home because he says it's a place of no opportunity and poverty and high crime and teen moms. He's looked at the statistics. He grew up in Raleigh. He's a city boy. But he says he loves my brain. "It's your brain that got you out of there Maddy," he says to me. We met in Honor's World Lit first semester freshman year.

I didn't answer because I'm mad at him anyways. He's obsessed with this old house downtown and won't take me to go see it. And he won't stop going on and on about it.

He was standing in my room just a couple nights before I came home, telling me about it, freaking me out. He told me he'd been going to see this house every night I wasn't with him. He said he'd been doing it for like three weeks. He said he needed to see it before he went to sleep. He told me he'd even gone to the state records and looked up the names of everyone who'd lived in the house. Then he'd gone to the cemetery and did gravestone rubbings of everyone whoever lived in the house. When he was in my room the other night he showed me one, rolled it right out on my bed.

"Here," he said. "I want you to have it."

But he couldn't tell me why—him, out of all people, who knows the reason for everything—he couldn't tell me why he had to look at that house at night. The way he looked at me. I'd never seen anyone look like that before. He said, "I wish I could tell you why."

He said at night when the moon is in the center of the roof of the house across the street, the moonlight shines in a high window on the house and you can see the spiral staircase that leads up to the widow's walk.

I asked him to take me and show me and he said he couldn't do it.

Waiting in the truck, I watched the people going in and out of Walmart. And I did see teen moms and one of them was wearing a COAL ASH PLANT = JOBS shirt and I knew it wouldn't do any good to tell her any different, to tell her I know this because I'm in college—a place she can't afford to think about because she's got a baby she's toting and caring for and if she needs that Coal Ash Plant job what do I tell her? Patrick's right about where I'm from.

And I saw myself like I was a character in a movie. My daddy's an alcoholic tig welder. His girlfriend has wire rose tattoos. Her son isn't afraid of snake bites. And I was sitting in the Walmart parking lot in a town with a big water tower. Nothing out from it except fields and fields, and woods for two hours until you got to a place with a mall or movie theater. And you just keep going from there until you end up in a big city where people don't care who you're holding hands with.

Maybe everything would have been alright if I'd been from

the city. Mama would have been able to love me somewhere like that. That makes sense to me. But that's not how it happened.

I wanted to think about something else, so I pulled to the edge of the lot under a tree and I got to it quickly. I closed my eyes I started thinking about Cammie's breasts, how they'd feel heavy in my hands. I was still wet from where I was before, moving my hand in circles. Then everything got dark and a light shined on Queenie in the corner, she was scared in a little ball, her scales moving with her breath. I moved harder then, tried to think about something else, focused on my fingertips, the pressure building, I moved faster, tried to figure how to get to it. I felt my body getting stiff but I was rising. I was pushing my heels off the floor. Cammie's erect nipple, then Patrick putting his fingers in my mouth. And right before I could tell it was happening, I saw Mama and Daddy in bed. She was laughing, licking his face. I came then like something so big had come out of me. I heard myself crying, and I was. I didn't want to but I couldn't stop. I couldn't help it.

When I saw Daddy and Cole coming I looked in the glovebox for napkins to wipe the smell off my fingers. I threw the napkins outside like real trash. Daddy and Cole hopped in and they asked me what was wrong. I told them it was an eyelash and handed Cole his new game.

"Alright!" Daddy said. "Heeeere it is!" Like we'd discovered some long awaited continent.

"Yep," I said, trying to chip in. I rubbed my eyes and started the truck.

The whole ride home Cole was steady talking about it his new game but every once in a while he would pat my knee. "You can build castles and houses. And secret hideouts. You can build anything you want. Put gardens and lakes and sheep anywhere you want." Cole said it all real quick and the open fields went on forever around us. Daddy told me to slow down for deer even though we didn't see any. And we all made a pact not to tell Rhonda about the bite.

When I put garlic powder on the toast for dinner Daddy made a joke about how that's something I've picked up in the city, something I've been learning on that fancy scholarship. He told me he knew I was busy up there but that he missed me and I should call him more often.

We put all the cheese we could find on our Hamburger Helper. We ate in front of the TV. Daddy said what he always says, "This is better than anything you'll get in a restaurant." He called Rhonda all giddy to tell her how good everything was going.

We ate like we've never eaten before. Daddy drank out of his shrimp cup, the little pink shrimp shook his booty, and I made myself some medicine too. Queenie came out of her ball and we watched Cole build the world he wanted. He was making a place with a candle beside every bed.

I leaned into Daddy on the couch and he wrapped me under his shoulder. I listened to the music from the game and thought what it would have been like to be my Daddy left with a little girl in a house at the edge of the woods. I kept drinking and closed my eyes and just listened. And I heard Daddy say, "This here is a pretty place. You've made a pretty place."

The Locket

Krystal has the most beautiful dive I've ever seen. I pull out the radio from the storage room and put it on the bucket behind the diving board. I don't turn it on because when Krystal gets in, she'll put it on WQDK 97.5, Today's Country Hits. She knows all the songs. And she sings and does her head from side to side like a real star. Sometimes she'll mess up, but then she'll just laugh. She's sixteen.

Sixteen is when you go to prom. I like thinking about prom. I didn't go to prom but Mother took me to Belk's anyway to try on dresses. The dress I picked had big poofy layers of blue chiffon and Mother brought me long white gloves to try on with it. And I spun around in that big floor to ceiling mirror. And then Mother laughed at me and told me not to be silly. She said that no one would ever ask me to prom, no one would ever ask me to anything. Mother was always right. She said the only thing I could do was ride a horse.

Norma was my best and only friend until she died. I have a picture of us on my nightstand. It's from when we won best in dressage at the state championship in '58. Mother made us matching color bows, peach colored! That picture is my favorite.

Sometimes I can hear Norma tell me things from heaven. She's been trying to get me to talk to Krystal. She says Krystal will be a good friend for me and she thinks Krystal's favorite animal is horses too. So today I'm going to try to talk to her. I'm just so shy!

The sun's not out yet. But I put on my first layer of sunscreen. UV rays can come through the clouds. And then I set up my green chair next to the picnic table. And once I do that my first layer of sunscreen has dried, so I put on my second. And then I put on my big favorite sun hat and take out my water bottle and get settled in my chair.

The pool looks pretty and clean and I am proud of myself for doing a good job. I am happy that the town lets me be the custodian for the pool. It's a nice job for someone like me, my age of 60. I think that maybe later when it warms up, I might go for a swim. I go sit at the edge of the little end and stick my legs in the water. I'm moving them around making swirls when I hear the front gate open and close. And I look up and Krystal's there in a big old sleep shirt. Her hair is piled up on her head like she just woke up. And she's alone. She doesn't have the twins she's been watching all summer. They must be at the beach or somewhere on vacation. It's just me and her here at the pool today.

"Hey, Miss Shirley," she says.

I get up and go back to my green chair. And she puts her bag down on the picnic table. I can see her legs have goosebumps.

"Hey," I say.

She steps out of her flip flops in a turn and then goes to the pool to dip her foot in the water. She always tests the pool like that before she gets in. And then she walks back over to the picnic table and asks me if I put the chemicals in the pool the first thing in the morning when I get there or before I leave in the afternoon. She says she read in *Seventeen* magazine that the chemicals make your hair less shiny.

I want to tell Krystal the truth, but I also want her to stay.

"A little white lie is okay," Norma says to me from heaven.

So I tell Krystal I put the chemicals in it in the afternoon.

"Good," she says and she takes off her sleep shirt in one graceful sweep.

And oh my gosh! She's wearing a bikini I've never seen before. It's peach!

Norma says, "Just like our bows! She's got style!"

She heads to the radio and bends down in front of it instead of crouching. She puts it on the country station and after she gets the volume just like she likes it, she spins back around singing. She comes back over to the picnic table and takes the bobby pins out of her hair and it uncurls in this one big amber fall down her back. She's got pretty hair. I've always thought so. She shakes it out a little and pulls her peach bathing suit out of her butt cheek as she goes to the diving board. And then she runs to the end of it and bounces and dives. It's so quick and perfect. Don't even make much of a sound.

When she comes up her hair looks very long and soft and she smooths it back with her hands. And then she wipes her eyes.

I can see her class ring glittering above the water. It must be from her sweetheart. He's probably very handsome. I bet he's the quarterback.

"I bet he's in the Volunteer Fire Department," Norma says.

Krystal pulls herself out of the pool instead of using the ladder. The water trickles down her legs. And her hair runs straight down her back. She turns towards the diving board so fast that water spins out from her. I want to tell her how wonderful of a dive that was. I have to tell her. Norma would want me too. After Krystal passes I tell her, "That was a beautiful dive." She turns her head around quickly and she's smiling. "Well, thank you," she says. And then she joins in with the chorus of the song. *She's in love with the boy. She's in love with the boy. She's in love with the boy. And even if they have to run away she's gonna marry that boy someday.*

Krystal dives again and it's more beautiful than the last. It seems that every one of them is that way. And I think I could watch her for hours.

By the time Krystal takes a break, it's the afternoon and the sun is right on top of us. She puts big fancy sunglasses on and spreads out her big zebra towel next to me. She gets some quarters out of her big pool bag and heads to the drink machine. She asks me if I want a Pepsi. And I say, "No thank you." But I am glad she asks.

She comes back from the drink machine drinking her Diet Pepsi. And by the time she gets to me, she's already finished it. She takes her suntan lotion out and starts smoothing it on her shoulders and arms, then her belly and legs. And I wonder if I should ask her if she'd like me to put some on her back. If I was Krystal's best friend, I could put suntan lotion on her back.

She puts the lotion back in her bag and pulls out a pack of Virginia Slims and a lighter.

"Can you keep a secret, Miss Shirley?" she says.

I nod and pull down my sunhat.

"Don't want my folks to know I smoke," she says as she lights the cigarette. She sits Indian style, facing the pool, and flicks the ashes in the Diet Pepsi can like an expert. "It's nice not having those twins today," she says, with her back to me. "I've been needing a break real bad," she says. The smoke slowly comes out from her. And it doesn't smell really strong and nasty like most cigarettes. And her hair starts to dry in the sun. I bet her hair don't tangle.

Norma's hair never tangled. She loved me to wash it behind the barn. I special ordered her strawberry shampoo. It made pink bubbles. And nobody believed me, but sometimes when we'd ride together in the summer, Norma's hair would shine pink.

"Oh, I forgot to ask," Krystal turns around to me. "Would you like one?" She leans her head towards her cigarette.

Norma says, "Yes, try it Shirley! Don't be a square!"

But I say, "No, thank you."

"That's okay," Krystal says and she lifts her hair off her back. She's starting to sweat, I can see it sparkling on her. She's so tan. I've never been that tan in my life. "I didn't think you smoked," she says.

Norma says, "Talk to her some more! Be her friend!" I can almost feel her nose nudging me.

So before Krystal turns around from me again, I ask her if she likes horses.

"They're my favorite animal," she says.

"I told you so," Norma says.

"My mama said you used to be a champion horse rider. That's so cool." Krystal scooches closer to me on her towel. "How many horses did you have?"

So I tell her how my family always had them, but never more than four at a time. But that Norma was the best, the prettiest, the fastest, the most graceful.

Krystal blows out smoke like an angel, like she's puckering up for a kiss. She asks me what color Norma was.

And I tell her sable brown, and how she was a direct descendant of Sir Archie, the father of the American thoroughbred. And how I started training her when I was twelve and how by the time I got to be her age we were making the papers. And I probably tell her a lot of other things that I can't remember. Then I stop and see that I'm talking with my hands like Mother always makes fun of me for doing. So I put them together on my lap like a nice young lady.

Krystal takes a last drag and stubs out her cigarette on the top of the Diet Pepsi can and sits it off her towel.

"Norma sounds beautiful," she says and she scooches closer. "To tell you the truth, even though they're my favorite animal, I really don't know that much about horses, but I've always wanted to ride one." She starts biting at a hangnail. "I guess because they always look so free when they're running fast. Or maybe it's just a little girl fantasy, you know?" She rips the nail and spits it beside her and then looks up to me. "I used to have horse posters all in my bedroom."

"I know you'd be a natural rider," I say. "I bet Norma would have loved for you to ride her." I think that Norma would have loved for Krystal to ride her fast in the fields in the morning mist.

Krystal puts her legs under her and straightens her back and asks me what kind of necklace I'm wearing. "I love jewelry," she says.

And I can't believe I've forgotten, but I suppose I do wear it every day and I never take it off. I'm wearing the locket Mother gave me when Norma died. It has her hair in it. But I just tell Krystal it's my special locket.

"Cool," Krystal says. "Can I see it?"

I have never shown it to anyone. I get a little afraid.

"Well, I would but the clasp is so small," I say. "It's really hard to get off. My arthritis as it is."

And before I know it, Krystal hops up and she's behind me taking off my favorite sun hat. Krystal's fingers feel warm and soft on my neck. Her fingernails almost make me tingle. I close my eyes and feel the locket come off my chest.

When I open my eyes, Krystal is standing in front of me, holding the locket open in the sun.

"Hey Shirley, look over here," Norma says.

I turn and look in the yard beside the pool and Norma is there in the sun. I can't believe it! Her hair is blowing so pretty. I smile at her and she smiles back at me like she's proud.

"What you see?" Krystal says.

I turn around and Krystal's standing there moving the locket different ways in the sun.

"Oh, nothing," I say. I wish Krystal could see Norma behind me, but I know she can't.

But I do tell Krystal that she can borrow my locket anytime.

"Really?" she says and she holds it next to her heart. "Gosh, Miss Shirley I'd love that. I've never seen anything like this. This is really something special."

"Anything for a friend," I tell her.

And me and Krystal stay all afternoon at the pool. She dives and dives. And we get hot dogs from the Duck Thru across the street! We both get just plain with ketchup! And Norma watches us from under a tree. And I'm happy to be there with all my friends. And when Krystal leaves she waves goodbye to me and then touches my locket on her chest. And then I wave goodbye to Norma under the tree and she walks down the street towards the café. "See you later," I say.

When I walk into the door at home I feel like I am beaming, like my smile is so happy that the whole world can tell. Mother is sitting at the kitchen table waiting for me to make her tomato soup. She eats tomato soup at 4:30. She eats early because she is so old.

"Why are you grinning so dumb, child?" Mother says to me.

But I don't want to answer her.

"You don't have to," Norma says.

"The low sodium kind, and don't put any pepper, you know I can't stand spices." Mother pulls her sweater around her tighter. She struggles a little with the collar. I reach to help her but she pulls away.

I tell her I only buy the low sodium kind, and that I never use any pepper. The last time I did she coughed all night. I grab a can from the pantry and open it, pour it in the pot and turn the eye on.

"Put that eye on 3, Shirley," Mother coughs and reaches for the tissue box in the middle of the table. "How many of my fine French cooking ware have you ruined using that high heat?"

"But I'm only thinking of you, Mother," I say. "The hotter it is, the quicker it gets done and quicker you can eat."

I look outside the window and see another horse I have never seen before! It's an Arabian horse with a shimmering black coat. Its mane is decorated with beads! It's digging at the roots of the crepe myrtle with its hooves. I gasp.

"What's wrong with you, girl," Mother says.

I look down and I've already burned the soup.

"I'm sorry," I say. "I'm sorry." I don't want Mother to yell at me.

The black horse is watching me be afraid.

"Where is Norma?" I ask it.

"You idiot," Mother says behind me. "She's dead."

I get so mad that I take the pot of soup and throw it on Mother. She screams and I go lay down in my bed and listen to her screaming until it turns to coughing again. I put my pillow over my head, hold it against my ears. But I can still hear Mother start to call, "Help me!" she screams.

When I get up the black horse will still be out there digging. I'm afraid to ask it again where Norma has gone. But she can't be too far.

I'll tell Krystal about it tomorrow. She has to understand.

Sister

Sister's got mono. She's real sick. She's five and I'm seven. And Aunt Nell's taken her down to her house to stay. She says she's on "core-an-teen."

So Sister's down there staying in that bedroom our great-grandmama died in. She died before we were born but she was really sick too, she had sores all over her body and they oozed with blood and green pus. That's what Aunt Nell told me.

I ain't been in that bedroom much but I think great-grandmama's ghost is down there because it seems to me that's where a ghost like her would want to live. And now that's where Sister is, sleeping in her bed. But Aunt Nell says there's no such thing as ghosts, only angels.

◊ ◊ ◊

When we go in to see Sister in that bedroom we have to be real quiet and everything is dark. Aunt Nell's covered the windows with paper and tape and blinds and curtains because Sister cries when the light comes in. We whisper in there one at a time and the fan moves like it's hardly working. Sister looks like a baby swallowed in pillows. And the ends of the old bed posts look like pineapples. And I'm sitting in Mama's lap and she points at the fireplace and tells me when she was little she saw Aunt Nell beat bats out of it with a broom. There's an old painting on the wall of a castle by the sea. The waves are high and there aren't any trees or birds singing. It's chipping in the corner.

If I get too close to Sister I might get mono too. But I lean up on the bed and ask her if she's afraid in here and she says no. I ask her if she's seen an old lady ghost and she says no. I ask her if she likes the castle painting by her bed and she says no. She says her head hurts. Aunt Nell says it's a "my-grain."

I was still a baby when Sister was born so I don't remember it. Her birthday is May thirteenth. I miss her kicking me in the bed at night.

I don't like leaving Sister in that room. I bring her in June bug shells. She won't hold them because she's a little scared but she tells me to hang them on the lamp in the corner. It's the only light she likes to have on in the room. I take my time and hang them all real careful in a neat row. And Sister squints and sees them. She says they're her jewels. And it is so pretty and I want to fill the lampshade full of June bugs for Sister. Her birthstone is an emerald. Mine is peridot.

I dream that great-grandmama sits on the end of Sister's bed when she's sleeping. And in my dream great-grandmama's skin is clear with no sores or blood or pus. It glows like a nightlight.

Mama sleeps with me at night because I'm too afraid to sleep by myself. I don't want to wake up with someone sitting on the end of my bed. Mama says Sister will get better soon and come home but she can't tell me when.

Aunt Nell tells me not to bring Sister any more June bugs. I tell Aunt Nell to leave me alone she's my Sister and I want to see her by myself. I have to get up on my tiptoes but I have good balance and I get the castle off the wall real easy. I put it in Sister's lap and crawl up in bed with her and we pick at the painting. We start at the ocean and then the cliff and when we get to the castle Sister falls asleep. I get out of bed and it's a big mess. Dark flecks are all over Sister and the sheets.

Then I go to the end of the bed and ask Jesus to let Sister come home. When I open my eyes and look up I see that the ends of the bedposts ain't pineapples, they're really just magnolia blossoms before they bloom.

◊ ◊ ◊

I ask Aunt Nell where I was when Sister was born and she says I was there, but that I was too little when it happened for me to remember.

Aunt Nell says Sister's gonna grow up and have her own babies and have a good life. And I want to know how she knows.

And that's when Aunt Nell tells me about the night we buried Sister's afterbirth. The afterbirth is the last part of us that comes out of our mamas. And we have to bury ours out by the swamp field. Aunt Nell said we buried hers right next to mine right out back of her house.

I leave then, run out the back door and try to remember. I run to the swamp path, the birds fly up around me. I stop to catch my breath. I close my eyes and hear the summertime bugs in the grasses. I think real hard back to when I was a baby, so hard I start to feel how the rocks turned warm in my hands that night. The dirt smelled wet and I could see the moon in the bottom of that hole, shining on that afterbirth of Sister. I wanted to help, I put the rocks down in the hole easy. I didn't want to break that moon.

An Unspoken

Hal Parker runs out to his wife's hydrangea bushes. He's trying to scare away the neighbor's black Lab, Major. Hal claps his hands in front of him and shouts, but Major's already peeing on the bush. It seems to Hal that lately the dog just won't stay in his pen. Hal has watched him dig holes under it and even seen him climb over it once or twice.

Hal looks next door. His neighbor Corey Lane's Camaro is in the yard. He decides to tell Corey about his dog. As he knocks on the door and waits, Hal looks over the front of the house and thinks he should have talked to Corey about Major weeks ago. He also thinks the bricks need to be washed and the shutters need to be repainted. He knocks again and hears the floorboards creak on the other side of the door. Major is back at the hydrangeas.

Hal doesn't see Corey much. He doesn't go to church, he doesn't go uptown except to get gas, and, Hal thinks, he sure doesn't spend enough time in his yard. He's inspecting the overgrown boxwoods beside him when Corey opens the door.

The first thing Hal notices is that the young man looks rough, thinner than he's been. But he goes ahead and asks him how he's been doing.

"All right, I reckon," Corey says. He scratches a scab on his wrist. His hair is greasy.

"Well, I hear you been doing good work at Johnny's chicken houses. He's told us about it at the café," Hal lies.

"Really?" Corey straightens up a bit. "Sure did. Johnny's a good man, he'll take good care of ya if you keep on doing good."

Corey's scab starts to bleed.

"Lord knows it ain't the best-smelling work," Hal laughs.

Corey smiles a little.

"But shoot, you're probably used to it by now."

"Yes sir." Corey wipes the blood with the palm of his other hand. "I don't even notice it no more."

"Well, I'm glad you're doing good for yourself, Corey. I really am." Hal takes a step toward him. "But I came over here to talk to you about your dog. Now I don't know what you got going on with that dog pen, but he can't keep getting out and running all over."

Corey shakes his head in agreement without looking at Hal.

"I know Major don't mean to hurt nothing. But you know how much Clara loves her flowers, and we've been working out in the yard all summer."

"I'm sorry," Corey says, "I really am."

"Have you tried an electric fence yet?" Hal asks him and he

looks back at his yard. Clara's there squatting on the ground with Major, giving him long strokes down his back. His tail wagging.

When Fred and Jenny Lane moved next door, Clara was excited. The Lanes were young and happy. And Jenny was newly pregnant. Clara enjoyed watching her with her growing belly plant boxwoods and azaleas around the front of the house. Jenny emitted that glow all new mothers do and Clara found it intoxicating. She helped throw a baby shower for Jenny with some of the other women at her church's fellowship hall. And to this day, Clara remembers how gracefully Jenny opened her gifts, unwrapping the paper at the taped ends instead of tearing it apart. And how she saved all the bows and ribbons, saying how pretty each of them was as she set them aside.

Corey was just two years old when Jenny was T-boned by a transfer truck on Highway 35. They say she died instantly. And Clara watched over the years as Fred brought in women who came from people she didn't know. She watched them move in and out, sometimes bringing their own children, sometimes not. The toys would always be left out in the yard. And the boxwoods and azaleas overgrew. Clara thought that if Jenny could see it all she'd roll over in her grave.

Clara did what she could to help Corey. She babysat him whenever Fred needed, refusing payment. She took him to Vacation Bible School every summer. And she gave him five dollars for every good report card.

Clara encouraged Hal to spend time with Corey. "I think it would be nice," she said to him. But Hal never showed any interest.

◊ ◊ ◊

While Clara's at the grocery store, Hal cuts her Knock Out roses. He wants to have them in a vase in the kitchen for when she walks in the door. He's trying to make her happy. She used to scratch his back until he went to sleep. He does not know why she stopped doing that but he's not going to say anything, either.

Clara remembers trying to hold her baby when he died. He was going in and out of fits and convulsions. He was screaming louder than she'd ever heard before. He was perfect, but he'd been born with a hole at the bottom of his spine. And that was in 1964 and the doctors told her that he wouldn't live six months, but he made it to eight. Every night before she went to sleep Clara thought about when he'd die and she tried to prepare herself for it. She thought it would be a peaceful thing. She thought she'd hold her baby boy still and quiet as he went. But he would not stop screaming. She didn't know that he'd bend and fight, that he'd turn in her arms into an unright thing. She did not think the Lord's will would work that way.

She does not remember much from the funeral. But the preacher asked everyone to join him in singing "Jesus Loves the Little Children." And everyone joined hands in a circle around her. They all were crying and singing.

Hal brings a glass of water to Clara in the living room. She's drafting the Murfreesboro Historical Association's newsletter, jotting in cursive on a legal pad, her feet on the couch.

Hal settles in his chair and puts the Western channel on TV. "Now I'm not trying to stir you up," he says, "but it's going on about twenty years you've been secretary. Ain't I right?"

"Well, something like that," Clara puts down her pen.

"Just think, if you didn't have to give tours near 'bout every weekend in the summer, maybe we could get down and see my brother's place in Pensacola."

Hal retired from auto insurance ten years ago. He had been one of the top sellers in the district. Working to make his home with Clara the best it could be. Enough for a carport, a koi pond, and a fountain with an angel tipping water out of a vase.

"I'll think about it," Clara says and she picks up her pad.

"I know you don't believe it, but they'll survive without you."

Hal looks over to the built-in bar in the corner cabinet and thinks that he's a better man now, better than the drunk he was. He gets out of his chair and sits next to Clara on the couch.

Clara packs mashed potatoes and hamburger steak into some Tupperware and covers it all in brown onion gravy. Sometimes she brings Corey leftovers and he especially loves her brown onion gravy. She sets the Tupperware in a paper grocery bag with two tomatoes from her garden and a ziplock with two sugar cookies she'd made for their last women's auxiliary meeting at church.

Then she goes back to the sink to finish the dishes. She washes quickly because she wants to bring Corey his food before sundown. And she washes out of habit, not looking at what she's doing. Instead, she checks on her African violet sitting in the window in front of her. She'd just planted it in this bigger pot and she thinks that it's filling out nicely. It's early September, the window is open and there are sounds outside.

When Clara looks up Corey is fucking his dog, Major. They're together

in the dog pen and Corey is pushing Major into the dirt. The dog yelps, and Clara screams.

She closes her eyes and turns away from the window and she stands there in her kitchen feeling like she's been thrown.

Hal finds Clara standing with her wet hands in balled fists covering her eyes. She clutches a fork in one hand and a sponge in the other. Water and suds drip down her arms and onto her apron and the floor.

Hal says her name and asks her what's wrong but she won't respond or move. When Hal starts to unpry her fists, she says, "I saw him. I saw him."

"Who? Let go. Let's sit down. What's wrong? Clara! Clara!"

"I saw him." Clara shakes her head back and forth.

Hal grabs her shoulders and then Clara stops and unclenches her fists. The fork and sponge fall to the floor. She opens her eyes and with her palms open on either side of her face she says, "I saw him having sex with the dog." The first thing Hal thinks is that he wants to kill that son of a bitch.

The sun sets and Clara sits at the kitchen table. She looks at the refrigerator and sees the clipping of Corey she cut out of the paper when he was the valedictorian of his high school class. And then she starts to cry. "I always knew something won't right with that boy. He won't ever right." Hal grabs the phone on the wall.

"Not yet," Clara says, "don't call the law yet. Please, Hal." Hal stands there with the phone in his hand. "I've got to pray about it."

"Pray? You want to pray about it?"

"I know you've never showed any care for Corey as long as he's lived. He was just a poor child and you never wanted anything to do with him." Clara starts to wring her hands. "And you know just as good as me that he's done dwindled down to nothing. Since his daddy died, he don't have nobody."

Hal looks out the window.

"You told me yourself that the other night when you went over there he looked the worst that you'd ever seen him." Clara wipes her face. "This is gonna ruin him."

"He's already rurnt, Clara." Hal hangs up the phone and comes toward her. "Everybody knows he was runt from the start. Them Lanes were trash, but you never wanted to believe it."

"That's not true. You know that's not true. Corey is a good boy, Hal."

"With that lowlife daddy, dragging women from Arrowhead onto our street, stealing out of my shed. You know as good as me he was the one that stole my generator last Christmas, probably sold it for who knows what kind of drugs," Hal went on. "But you turned an eye. And don't you think I know that you give him money here and there for gas or shoes or whatever you think he needs whenever you go over there?"

Clara looks at the bag of food she got together for Corey sitting in the middle of the table.

"Clara, this has gone on long enough. It's time you faced the facts. That boy is sick and you can't save him." Hal puts his hands palms down on the table.

And outside Major starts to bark.

Even though their son was born "defected," Hal still named him after his father. Hal was proud to have a son. And doctors are just doctors, Hal thought, they can be wrong about a lot of things. His son could still grow to be strong.

When their son was dedicated to the church when he was five months old, Hal insisted on holding him in front of everyone. The mama always holds the baby during dedications, but Hal wanted to do it.

"What will you do if he gets upset and starts to fidget and all?" Clara asked, holding their son on the bottom church step.

"You'll be all right, won't you, bud?" Hal touched their son's nose.

"Now you have to make sure you hold him real gentle when the preacher sprinkles the water on him." Clara passed their son to Hal. "It might surprise him, scare him some."

"My son ain't gonna be scared," Hal said and he walked up the church steps with their baby.

Hal ended up being right about the dedication. He told everyone afterward that his son had acted like a little man. Later that night before they went to sleep Clara told Hal that she'd been thinking about what she wanted to bury their baby in. Hal had never wanted to yell at Clara before, but he wanted to then.

Clara looks over. Corey does not have his front porch light on. But the moon shines bright enough that she can find her way. She calls Major to her and she watches him move toward her from the edge of the darkness until the moon finds him and shines down his black coat. She squats down and takes his head in her hands. She holds him there and looks into his eyes and prays. She listens and waits for God's quiet voice. Major breathes warm and heavy onto her and then he jerks his head to sniff into the bag of Corey's leftovers. Clara gets up and gives Major a sugar cookie. And she watches him take it back into the dark.

Clara prays all the way to Corey's door. She knocks and the porch light comes on. She waits for God to tell her what to do and the door opens.

"Hey, honey," Clara says, "here's some leftovers for you."

She does not want to look at him, but she hands him the bag. "Hamburger steak with that brown onion gravy you love so good."

The overhead light is swirling with bugs.

"Thank you, Miss Clara," Corey says.

And Clara tries to smile.

"You're welcome," she says and she turns to leave. "Now go on in and eat. Put some meat on them bones."

"Miss Clara," Corey stops her.

She turns and looks up to him from the bottom step of the porch. And for a moment he doesn't say anything. The swirling bugs make strange shadows on his face. And his eyes look like deep holes in his head.

"Miss Clara, I... I heard you scream earlier. I know you saw me. And I'm so sorry, I'm so, so sorry... "

His voice breaks.

◊ ◊ ◊

"Yes," Hal says into the phone, "you heard me right. He was fucking his dog. Corey Lane."

The police tell Hal they'll come get Major the next morning and even though it'll be Sunday, this is a special case.

Hal tells the police everything he can think of about Corey. He's a druggie, a thief, a dog fucker. And while he talks he looks out the window and there under Corey's porch light, Clara's in the dog fucker's arms.

When Hal and Clara got married, Clara's cousin suggested that they go to Pecan Grove for their honeymoon. It was a quaint resort hotel the county over, with little bungalows on the river. "Just big enough to spit in," Clara's cousin said, "love shacks."

Hal knew Clara was a virgin. He knew he'd have to be slow, but he hoped eventually she'd learn to be wild. He remembers thinking about this while he tried to make love to her that night. How he could wrap her long hair around his fist, pull her head back, take off her clothes. But all she wanted to do was look at the river. Jumped out of the bed to go stand at the window. She would not stop talking about how pretty the stars were reflected on the water. How it was the most beautiful thing she'd ever seen. How they made different colors, not only silver but gold and sometimes purple, too. She pulled him off the bed, put him next to her.

"See," she said, pointing into the night.

"Yes," he said. But he didn't see the stars on the river. He wanted to.

At first Clara was proud that Hal was making enough money to put a bar in their home. She thought that's what nice family homes had. He built it in the corner cabinet in their living room, with glass shelves, silver rimmed tumblers, and fancy track lighting.

But soon after, when she'd come home from substituting, or leading a historic tour, or planting crape myrtles on Main Street, she'd find Hal slurring his words. And then she found him standing in the hall. He was in front of the pictures of their dead baby, the ones that were taken at the nice portrait studio, where all the families went to take pictures of their pretty children. And when the photographer saw that Hal had made a special wedge out of sponge so the baby could sit up without his back hurting, the photographer kept saying, "What a happy baby," over and over again. And Clara put a white fuzzy blanket over the wedge to make it softer. And it almost looked like a little lump of snow.

And that time when Clara found him drunk, he turned to her and slung his arm down the hall lined with pictures of their dead baby. "You should have never put these up here and you know it," he said, "I got to see them every damn day. Our pretty baby smiling."

In her whole life of being in the church, Clara had never asked for an unspoken. It was a rare request, reserved for those who were brave enough to ask for prayers about the unspeakable. But after she saw Hal in the hall that day, in front of all the pictures, she wanted to ask for one. But she knew as soon as she did, everyone would know that something was wrong. So she did not ask for an unspoken because she was ashamed of him.

Hal waits on the porch with coffee, watching down the corner for the police. He hears a gunshot from Corey's house and looks over and sees Corey standing over Major in the pen with a shotgun.

Clara runs out on the porch, eyes wide with fear.

Hal catches her.

"It was Major," he says, "Corey shot him."

"I thought it was Corey." Clara shakes in Hal's arms.

"I know," Hal says.

He holds her and hopes that Corey buries Major good enough that the stray dogs don't dig him up and strow him in his yard.

At church when the preacher asks, "Are there any more prayer requests?" Clara raises her hand and says, "I have an unspoken."

As soon as Clara puts her hand down, Hal puts his on top of hers. He whispers, "I'm proud of you."

She pulls her hand out from under his and whispers, "It wasn't for me."

She looks ahead of her at the way the morning light comes through the tops of the tall windows. How it hits the stained-glass Jesus behind the baptismal pool. He's standing with his arms open in a meadow. Baby sheep are sleeping at his feet. And when the preacher says, "Let us pray," Clara closes her eyes. She bows her head.

Uncle Elmer

When me and Sister were little Uncle Elmer took us to Wendy's because they have the biggest senior citizen discount, and we didn't know what that meant, but somehow, we knew that meant cheap because this was a word he loved to say: cheap. I can get that for cheap at Sam's he'd say. He wore a cap that said READ THE INSTRUCTIONS with a picture of an open book that said THE HOLY BIBLE and he played the guitar and made us sing "Power In The Blood" because it was the only song he knew how to play. And he held us too long when he hugged us real tight, and he made me sit on his lap, and it wasn't until my first kiss hundreds of miles away when I was eighteen, sitting on a couch made out of leather, that I remembered Uncle Elmer licked my ear too. And I didn't say anything to anyone about it. See, he'd tell us at Wendy's that when he was born in Georgia his mama didn't want a boy, so she sent him to school in bonnets and dresses, told everyone he was her little girl. He fought in Germany in World War II, got married and had two children: one became a jewelry thief, and the other one married a woman who believes Jesus had blue eyes. He lived in Virginia Beach and he drove with one foot on the gas and the other on the brake pedal. He wore shirts that showed his chest hair—it was black. He took us to the mountains. He took us to the mall. He paid us for picking up pecans in his yard. At Wendy's, he'd dump whatever crust was left of his French fries out the box and onto a napkin and then lick his finger and pick up every piece of salt. After my Aunt Lillie died, he married a woman in the Philippines, much younger with children and dreams of an American college. He flies over to see her, navigating the overcrowded streets in his tennis shoes from before I was born. He sends us a picture of Philippine string beans—they're real skinny and long. He takes out his hearing aids and has sex with his new wife, and when they're done he takes her family out to Wendy's, and he licks his finger again.

The Bass

I know I can get better if I want to. Everybody can get better if they want to.

At the Duck Thru the black ladies are talking 'bout the Bradley man that used to be sheriff in Halifax County. He killed himself yesterday. Melissa's rescue squad was called out to it. They say he called 911 and told them he was having chest pains. And by the time Melissa and them got there he'd shot himself in the chest with his sawed-off 12 gauge. He was still alive when they found him. Wallowing right there in his recliner. Melissa said he'd sold everything in the house except for that recliner. Like he'd been getting ready for it for months.

The black ladies are making sausage biscuits. And all Krystal's doing is looking at me.

"Right wet out there ain't it, Donnie?" she says.

I nod and rain falls off the end of my hat.

She giggles and leans on the counter, pushes her breasts together.

I ask her for a can of Grizzly, and she bends over like she's stretching. And I wonder for a minute what she'd be like, how she likes it. Me taking her from behind. Wrapping that white blond hair round my hand one good time. And it's alright. She's been acting like she wants me to be thinking about it—going on a while now. Since she turned up at our church, bringing them kids to Vacation Bible School.

She puts the can on the counter and says, "I won't tell Melissa." Melissa put me on the prayer list Sunday. Her cousin just got mouth cancer so she thinks I will too.

Krystal clicks her fingernails on the lighter case, her pointer finger has a little diamond in it. "Just got 'em done yesterday. You like 'em?" She holds out her hands in front of me, wiggles her fingers.

Before I can answer, she turns to them ladies, smiles at them and says, "Miss Gretchen and Hilly think they're gaudy but anyways..." She turns back to me and bangs the register with her fist to open it. She hands me my change, her bracelets clinking. "You got a plumbing snake? Melissa said she thought y'all did. I think one of my boys done put a truck in the commode."

"Don't worry 'bout it," I say. If I don't help Krystal, I'll hear it from Melissa so I tell Krystal I'll come over 'round five.

Krystal tells me to call her before I head over. She writes her number on the back of my receipt. I put it in my pocket without looking at it.

When I walk out the door them women are trying to figure if the Bradley man is gonna have an open casket.

"If he don't look too bad, then they ought to do it," one of 'em says.

"It's the right thing to do…for the family," says the other one.

I sit in the truck some and watch the cars fly down Highway 258. Flinging puddles out the road. 'Fore I even went out to the MacDaniel farm this morning, I knew it was gonna be a swamp. All that corn won't be worth five cents. Count of that tropical depression, rain's been here all week. I can't do nothing. But I pull out my phone and call Wayne anyway like a damn piece of shit 'cause me and Melissa need the money now with another baby coming. I call him and ask him does he want me to do anything out there on the MacDaniel farm. If there is any work I can do on that old picker in his shop. Wayne says he wishes he can help me, but he'll have me back in the field once the rain lets up. He tells me to tell Melissa he says, "Hello."

And right now she's rubbing her belly so happy. And right now I'm sitting here alone outside the Duck Thru in my truck and one thing I can always do right is count the teeth on this Grizzly can. That bear comes out having five teeth every time you count it. I put in a good dip. Hell, when me and Melissa was youngins she'd dip too. Don't know if she really enjoyed it, or if she was just trying to show off to all us on the baseball team. But she'd put a dip in bigger than anything you'd seen and sit right there on the tailgate looking just as pretty as you please, swinging her legs, telling us how she loved the tingle of it.

Now she's bought them special vitamins for having healthy babies. It's the first thing she does every morning. Takes that bottle from her nightstand and pops them vitamins and looks at me and grins.

It didn't even feel like nothing when I made that baby with her. I thought it would feel different but it just felt like every other time.

If I sit here too long folks'll see me sitting here. Don't want anybody to think anything. I just want something to happen. Or get caught up in something until something does. Wish I could just go to sleep and wake up and feel like there's something to look forward to.

I get out the truck and dig through all the shit in the truck bed. I find my cane pole and cooler and figure I'll go out to the pond. Long as I know my family's been fishing in this pond back off behind Slade Store Road. It's real nice, lots of pin oaks and gumball trees round the edges. A big Magnolia so old the roots rise up out the ground and you can sit there on 'em. Don't nobody ever come out there. Nobody to look at, nobody to look at me.

Daddy always said there was a bass out there but I ain't never seen one. Pond's too small for a bass. My daddy worked for Wayne's daddy. That's how that works. Won't until I was grown that I realized Daddy half-assed everything. Hell, he half-assed everything. He always told me he learned everything he knew from his daddy. I never knew the old man, he died before I was born. But I heard my daddy's old man hollered at him from the time my daddy was a baby. Scared Daddy so much he didn't talk until he was five years old.

Reckon that's why my daddy did some things to me too. I tell Melissa sometimes at night, before we sleep, and she listens and tells me it's alright. Melissa's too good a woman for me.

Soon as I pull down in there, I spit out my dip and I find the Rich and Rare in my glovebox. It's the best Canadian whiskey that's bang for your buck. I drink till the rain lets up to a drizzle and it feels like time is moving easier. And the rain looks like static on the pond. I get out and catch some crickets easy. I catch me a couple baby brim with the crickets, and bait the brim for a damn bass. I throw in round the edges and start jigging the line. A bass would be something.

Truth is, before our baby came, I came out here and swam out to the middle of that water. Went right in with my boots on. I wanted the water to fill me up till there won't nothing left. I wanted something to come and just pull me to the bottom. But I just floated there all afternoon and watched the sky change to stars. I was waiting there when I heard Melissa calling for me. I watched the light she was shining on the water, watched it get closer to me. She was screaming my name, running down into the water with her big belly, pulling me out. Telling me she loved me over and over and I couldn't say nothing. She was pulling stuff out of my hair and beard. Then she stopped and showed me. "Look, forsythia blooms," she said.

The line tugs and then pulls hard like a snatch and I know, I can feel it. It's a bass. And he's fighting too, boy. I get him to where I can see his eyes and get him on the shore. His stripe is pretty and straight. He's got to be about eight pounds.

I lay him in the tall grass, watch his gills open and close. He moves his fins real pretty. And he's bleeding from where he swallowed the hook. And looking at him like that, I almost don't want to keep him. But I sit there and watch his mouth move till the blood stops coming out of him. And I can't hardly believe it all. My fucking daddy.

I fill the cooler up with water and put him down in it easy.

◊ ◊ ◊

My watch says quarter till four. But I figure I'll call Krystal up anyway, get on over there a little early. And I don't know how she did it, but the way Krystal curled the "y" on her name looks like a damn heart, like some bullshit. I know she lives in Arrowhead but don't know which trailer is hers. I call her up and she tells me she lives at the back edge, in the blue singlewide. The one with the baby pool she says.

Only time I ever been out to Arrowhead was when Wayne's son asked me to bring him out here to buy some drugs from Big Bay Odom. I pass Big Bay's trailer and him and all them are sitting out in their yard watching me, smoking with their shirts off. When I pull up to Krystal's all these cats go running out from everywhere. And all her kids are watching me from the window, all those little heads, one on top of the other.

I grab the plumbing snake out the truck bed. And I check on the bass and his gills are still opening and closing. He'll probably be dead by the time I look at him again, suffocate in that water. I put in another dip and I hear Krystal yell at the kids. She flings open the front door and hollers, "Don't be a stranger Donnie, come on in the house." She's in a top she's about to fall out of. I know then what all this is gonna be. I look back towards Big Bay Odom's. They're still watching me. I can feel them watching me when I step into Krystal's trailer. She hugs me and thanks me for coming over and her kids all go stand in front of the couch. There's four of them, a boy 'bout twelve, two middle ones—a girl and a boy, and a baby. They all have white blonde hair like her. The place smells like cat piss.

"Y'all 'member Mr. Donnie don't ya?" She tugs at her shirt

to show more of her breasts. "He's the one that cuts the grass at church."

The middle girl starts to pick her nose.

Krystal pops her hand.

"What's that?" The oldest points to the plumbing snake in my hand.

"A plumbing snake, ain't that a funny name?" Krystal says.

"Don't look like a snake to me," the middle girl says.

They giggle and she tells them to go play in their room. The oldest one looks back at me and follows the rest of them ripping down the hall. Krystal leads me to her room and hollers at them to make her some more pictures. And I look back at the fridge and it's already covered in paper, every one of them is pictures of horses. Horses running in fields, on the beach with big suns over them. She'll have to take some down to make room for more.

Krystal's bed is made up with velvet-looking pillows that say "Angel." She picks one up and squeezes it against her. Her skin looks glittery. "Got these from the Dollar General," she says. "Can you believe it? They're getting more cosmopolitan all the time."

"Yeah," I say. "Where you want me to put this plumbing snake?"

"That sink there's fine," she points behind me to her bathroom.

There's a big picture of Marilyn Monroe blowing a kiss above the commode and Krystal's got a candle lit in front of the bathroom mirror, smells like cotton candy. It's next to a pink ashtray slam full of butts. It's a glass one, looks antique. I tell her that most folks think you need a plumbing snake when they just need a plunger.

"Well I tried the plunger already. All day yesterday I was trying that plunger." She comes into the bathroom and lights a Virginia Slim with a flowery lighter. She edges up on the counter and sits her lighter by the candle.

"I've been having to use the kid's bathroom," she says. "And with all of them, it's right crowded." She flicks her cigarette into the ashtray. "'Bout like living in the old days," she laughs.

"I reckon," I say.

I grab the plunger from behind the commode and while I'm plunging, I can see her out the corner of my eye, tracing her knees with her diamond fingernail. I can feel whatever that's in the commode give and I spit my dip out in it. I give it a flush and it unclogs just fine.

"Well, that won't much of nothing," she says and she stubs out her cigarette.

"I don't think it was a toy, coulda just been a lot of paper," I say.

She gets down off the counter and wiggles her toes into the pink rug. "I knew it, I've been telling Jeenie to stop using so much paper, but she likes using my bathroom. What can I tell her? She's my only girl."

Krystal is acting dumb but she knows what she's doing. I study her feet. She's picked every one of her toenails down into the quick. There's dried blood in the corners of some of 'em.

"You just don't know how much I appreciate it," she says. She comes closer. "It's hard here you know. I need all the help I can get." She runs her fingers down my shirt buttons. Her nails make a sound when they touch my buttons. Like a clink like a tap.

"And I know you need some help too sometimes. Let me make you feel better, Donnie." And she puts a finger into my shirt between the buttons, scratches my chest. "I know you've been hurting," she says, "for a long time."

And I'm caught up in it. I don't have no control. I pick her up and put her on the counter and rake my teeth down her neck, all the way down to her collarbone. Her nails go into my shoulders and her heels go into my ass. I shove my hand under her bra and her breasts are hot and soft at the same time. I pull off her top, rip down her bra. I bite her nipples and she clinches harder, gasps.

"You like it hard, don't you," Krystal says.

I throw her on the bed. She gets up to reach for me and I pull her legs out from under her. She gets up again and I grab her hair, wrap it 'round my hand one good time.

"You're a bad man, Donnie Dunlow," she says.

I stand there and hold her out from me on the bed and she likes that. She's wiggling out of her jeans, flinging them to the corner of the room. She's making good noise. I want to feel her shaking while I'm inside her. So hard inside her.

"That's right, I am a bad man," I tell her.

She's trying to reach for me, clawing for me like it's all she knows how to do.

"Fuck me, Donnie." She gets louder. "I said I want you to FUCK me."

A kid starts screaming, comes flying down the hall. And the bedroom door starts beating, the doorknob shaking, turning so fast.

I let go of Krystal's hair and she falls on the bed. The bathroom light makes my shadow on her. She turns over to face me and I see now all of her naked body. Her chest heaves, her legs stretch.

"I'll be there in a minute, Baby," she yells to the door. She starts to get up and stops in front of me, looks at me like she's about to cry.

I'm back where I started and I can see everything now for what it is. And all I can do is slap her. I slap the shit out of her, slap her as hard as I can.

I pick her hair out from 'round my fingers and watch the beating door. When I open it the middle girl's standing under me wringing her hands.

"Tell them to stop chasing me with that spider," she points down the hall.

They're all looking at me from the end of the hall. But I still wipe my face and pull myself together. And I tell them I gotta bass in the back of my truck.

Heading out the trailer the cats come up underneath my feet, 'bout to damn trip me. The baby runs straight into the baby pool, fast as lightning. Even with all the rain it still looks like the water's been standing in it for months. The middle girl grabs him, wipes the green shit off his fat little legs. The boys crawl up the sides and lean in over the truck bed. I open up the cooler, and he don't look the same anymore. He don't look as beautiful. He's starting to die.

"Now that there is the prettiest bass I've ever seen!" The oldest takes a picture of him on his phone. "You'll have to take me with you next time man."

One of the cats jumps in the truck bed, looks like it's got a stomach full of worms. The oldest boy picks it up and starts scratching its head.

"Lookee!" The girl holds up the baby and the baby sticks it's head in the cooler.

The bass moves his tail fin and barely makes the water slosh. The cat perks up. The baby squeals. It's right pitiful.

"What you gon' do with him, Mithter Donnie?" The middle boy has a lisp. "He's so big, he'd liable to take up the whole wall!" He holds his hands out real wide above his head and the rest of them laugh.

I look out towards Hertford County and it looks like another storm cloud is coming. It'll be raining again soon. I tell the kids to head back in the house. And Big Bay Odom and all the trash sitting in their front yards, smoking cigarettes in Arrowhead, sees me leave out of there.

I sit in the truck outside my house and I tell myself that I caught a bass and that my wife will be happy. And that I am a good man coming home to my family. I am a good man.

When I walk in the house, first thing Melissa says to me is, "Where's the diapers?"

She hits the side of the skillet with the spoon and puts her other hand on her hip, "I told you this morning 'fore you went out that Bailey needs some more diapers."

Bailey's on the floor reaching for her Mama with cheerios stuck to her chest.

I grab Melissa and kiss her on the mouth.

"Golly, honey," she says. "What's gotten into you?"

I tell her to close her eyes. I watch her a little there with her eyes closed wiping her hands on a dish rag. "Did you get them pork chops like I asked," she pushes a curl out her face.

I run and grab the bass out of the cooler and the baby laughs at me when I come in. And when I tell Melissa to open her eyes she is so happy. She says how special the bass is. She tells the baby her Daddy ought to go in the paper for a bass like this. I'm standing there in the kitchen holding it and I be damn if he ain't dead yet. His gills open and close so slow. Melissa don't even notice. She's kissing me, taking off my cap. She's taking a picture of me and him on her phone.

"I'll caption it: MY GREATEST CATCH," she says. She giggles at her own joke. She looks at me like she loves me.

"Let me put him down," I tell her. I put him on the cutting board and he lays there real still. We stand over him together and I put my hands around her waist.

"He's so pretty Donnie," she says. "You ought to mount him. We could put him above the TV!"

I watch him stop moving.

Melissa moves my hand to be on her belly. "We could mount him and put him in our little man's room," she says it so sweet like.

But I don't want to think about that. I tell her let's eat him. He'll be good and nice with all the vitamins and all that stuff our babies need. I can't believe how happy I sound saying it. And I rub her belly and she puts her hands on mine.

Melissa says she'll clean him, that she'll finish taking care of supper. She tells me I deserve it. I pour a glass of tea and I sit on the couch and look at the baby in front of the TV. Melissa keeps going on about the bass.

I scratch my beard and some glitter falls outta it. What did Krystal say to those youngins when they all jumped in front of each other showing her the horses they made for her? I don't remember. I watch the ice melt in my glass, watch the glass drip on the outside. It's gonna make a ring on the end table. I feel like the glitter is all over me. I feel like it's shining all over me. Then Melissa hollers for me.

She's standing there with blood on her hands.

"I can't do it," she says, "you're gonna have to get the head. His bones are too strong."

When I bring the knife down it feels like the rest of his body jerks. His backbone is so strong I have to really work at it until it breaks in two. Krystal said she knew I'd been hurting. I 'bout can't stand it.

Melissa puts her hand on my shoulder and then puts his head in a bowl in the sink.

And I go take a shower and get all the glitter and blood and everything off of me.

When Melissa says the blessing, she opens her eyes to me and rubs her belly.

"He just kicked," she says. "He's so excited about his Daddy's bass."

I know damn well that's not true. She's not even showing yet. But I feel excited that she feels excited. And that makes me feel like it's something I can smile about.

Melissa fries the bass perfect. And he's big enough for me and Melissa to split a filet. And she eats him like she's starving, like she's been waiting for him all along. It makes me feel good. In between mouthfuls she asks me what work Wayne had for me today, and I tell her nothing.

"Didn't even have nothing at the shop?" she says and pinches off some filet to give to the baby.

I shake my head.

The baby smooshes her fingers in the pretty white meat.

"Well, y'all will be out in the field soon enough." Melissa wipes the baby's face and hands. "Weatherman says this rain will be easing off soon."

I take my first bite and he don't taste musty or anything, cleanest fish I ever tasted.

"What about Krystal," Melissa says. "You get up with her?"

"Well, yeah," I say.

"You didn't charge her nothing did you?" Melissa says. "You know she can't barely afford any shoes for those kids."

I try to remember if those kids had any shoes on.

"I told the women's auxiliary that we need to take up a love offering for 'em." Melissa talks to the baby, getting her out of the highchair. "Ain't that right, sweet baby girl?" Then she stops and looks at me on her way from the table, "And you know what I'll put a plate together and you can take it to her tomorrow. We've got enough to feed an army."

I think of Krystal poking my bass apart with her fingernails, feeding all those youngins like little birds. Them underneath each side of her, reaching up with their open mouths.

"You're a good woman, Melissa," I say.

I clean off the table. And then I get the rest of my bass out the sink. I take him out and dump him at the edge of the yard.

Bailey sleeps in our bed between us. She don't move or wake up for nothing. Melissa thinks it's sweet.

Melissa puts her Bible down on her stomach and I can tell she's praying, praying for everybody, but I know she's praying for me. I've known that since she found me out there in the pond. And I know she wants to tell me that she knows that's where I caught that bass. But she won't say it because she don't want to hurt me.

"Don't forget the Bradley man's wake is tomorrow," she says.

I think about that Bradley man sitting alone in his recliner, alone in his empty house, in the middle of the afternoon. He probably had the blinds pulled. But he didn't want to be there for days until someone found him. Have his children come in and find him like that. That's why he called the rescue squad.

"Did he say anything when y'all got there?" I say. "I mean, was he able to talk?"

"Honey, I don't want to remember." She touches my cheek like a baby animal and then puts her hand on my chest.

"Well a man that kills himself ain't a man at all," I say. I feel like that's important for me to say. That's what my daddy said when L.G. Cook found out he had cancer and shot himself down one of his paths. That was the first time I remember knowing about anything like that.

"I think I'm proud of you, Donnie Dunlow," she says.

I can't do nothing but turn over away from her.

She tells me she loves me.

I look out and watch the rain start to hit the window and I tell her I love her too.

Melissa's pager goes off at about 11:45. She kisses the baby and is gone. I turn on the scanner on the nightstand and listen to her. She says there's a bad wreck out on Galatia Church Road.

Way off I can hear the sirens. I get my Grizzly from under the dresser and I slap it harder and harder. I put in my dip and look at my hands. I look at the back of them and I look at the front, I turn them over and over. I go to the gun cabinet and find half a bottle of Rich and Rare and sit it next to me. I spit out my dip and start to drink.

Melissa's still on the scanner. The baby's still asleep. And I sit and watch the rain go sideways, hear the lighting come. Next thing I know I near 'bout finish off the bottle.

I head out the house and it's so dark I can't see nothing. I walk into the push mower. It's already rusting, sinking in the mud. Every man ought to have a shed for his tools. But that don't matter now. The rain makes the bottle slip in my hands, but I drink it damn straight. Right there in my backyard, right there in front of the fields.

And don't you know the damn coons and dogs came out in the storm and took the last parts of my bass. I'm down on my hands feeling for him. I want to find where I broke him in two.

The Bear

Mama's sitting behind me on the porch telling me when to flip the salmon cakes. Like she can see when they're brown enough. Since she's been sick, she's been getting me to do more cooking. I'm old enough to do it by myself, I tell her. But she has to have it her way. Just like I know this one she's trying to tell me to flip ain't ready yet. It ain't brown like I want it to be on the bottom, I've been checking, but I do what she says anyways.

Mama's swatting flies. Don't know how they all get in the porch. Mama says Abner lets them in. And that don't make sense either. Everything's always Abner's fault with Mama and that ain't fair.

She says she got Daddy to screen in this porch so she could sit out here and enjoy it.

I turn around and watch her swat and kill another one. It was sitting on the arm of her rocking chair.

"That one there was a horsefly," she says.

She flicks it off her chair and looks out towards the swamp field.

I look too—the clouds back towards town look heavy.

"Looks like the bottom's gonna fall out," she says.

We all hope it does. We've been needing rain real bad. The corn's hurting, it won't be worth five cents. We've been praying for it at church. Worst dry spell we've had since I can remember. The animals don't even have any water. The creek down the swamp path has run dry. There's a bear that lives down there. We've seen him rambling for something to drink. He'll sway from ditch to ditch.

Wayne saw him last week laying in that fallow field next to Hiram's house. And he went up to him to see if he was alright. He figured the bear'd been hit on the highway. But when he got real close, the bear got up slow and went off real sleepy-like to the edge of the woods. Mama says he was probably laying out there to get cool, probably rolling in a patch of dirt. Mama says animals will act funny like that when they're dehydrated.

The dust comes up the path and Mama hollers through the porch window. She tells Sister to put ice in the glasses. I put the last salmon cakes on the platter and help Mama to the table. Daddy and Wayne and Abner come in to wash up. I pour tea in the glasses. Daddy tells Abner to wait for the blessing.

And Mama says the blessing, "For this and all your many gifts of love Lord, bless this to the nourishment of our bodies and our bodies to your service."

"And please send us rain," Daddy says.

"In Jesus' name we pray," Mama says.

And we all say, "Amen."

Abner is a grown man now, he's 25. But he smacks when he eats. And he never looks up at any of us. I can't stand it. And he ain't been getting any better. And he smacks so hard. Heaving forkfulls into his mouth, gasping for breaths in between. But Mama don't say nothing about it, she just talks over it. She asks Daddy if he got up with Donnie about cutting timber. She asks Wayne if he tended to the paint for the hunting lodge.

"Yes, Mama," they both say.

She's been asking them all week.

Mama tells Sister she did real good on the biscuits. Sister smiles but just for a second.

Abner grabs the bowl of butterbeans and almost spills them on the table.

"Slow down, son," Mama says.

Mama's always talked to us in orders.

Abner looks at Mama for the first time in a long time it feels like and then he looks back down at his plate. He asks me to pass him the salmon cakes.

Then Wayne says, "Well somebody's shot that bear."

I can't believe it. I don't want to.

"I found him out there in the middle of that fallow field," Wayne says and he reaches for his tea.

Wayne says he figures somebody rode by there and saw him wallowing in that dirt and thought he had rabies and called the law. Daddy says it was probably the new hot-to-trot sheriff, leaving that bear out there like that. His body out there swelling in the sun.

"Common," Mama says. "Common, if I've ever heard it."

"That bear was a pretty thing, too," Wayne says. He figures that bear was at least 300 pounds.

"You think he suffered?" Sister asks.

"He bled to death out there, I know that," Wayne says. "Shot him like they didn't know what the hell they was doing."

I started thinking about that bear waiting to die out there in that hot field.

"Funny that he stayed out there to die," Mama says. "Bears go off in the woods, find a thick patch of briar or a fallen tree to lay up under to die. They get in a ball up underneath something. I read it in the paper."

I look down at my salmon cake and it tastes good even though I didn't get it as brown as I wanted and I'm trying to finish my plate because Mama says there's folks out in the world that ain't got nothing to eat but I can't help it—I keep thinking about that bear.

When Abner was okay he read all these books about Indians. He told us at the dinner table one night that the Indians around here prayed to the bears for strength before big battles. And he told us that after an Indian died, his spirit stayed with his favorite arrowhead he made when he was living. And when Abner used to talk about the Indians so much I reckon he thought none of us was listening. But I was. And I wish he'd show me all those arrowheads he's got in his bedroom like he used to do. He'd tell me and Sister the story behind every one of em, what it killed and what it was made out of and how old it was and sometimes even how far it'd come from, all the way from Eskimos sometimes, places with snow and big mountains, big rivers and elks.

I look up at Abner and I want to tell everybody that it makes sense to me the bear was out there rolling around in the fallow field because he knew that's where he'd find arrowheads. And when he got shot, of course, he stayed out there to die because he wanted to die in the company of his friends, the Indian spirits. Maybe they were even singing him a song to get to Heaven.

But I don't say none of this because Abner pushes his chair back and it makes the table shake. He gets up and walks towards the sink and then he walks back to the kitchen table. He goes back and forth, wringing his hands over his knuckles, squeezing them, cracking them. They're starting to get red.

"Sit down, Abner," Mama says to him. "Now, come on and finish your dinner."

Daddy looks at Mama and says, "Let him be, Mama."

Then Mama says louder, "You know I thought I heard something this morning." She looks at Sister. "Didn't I tell you this morning that I heard a gunshot out towards Hiram's?" Sister nods her head yes, but everyone at the table knows that all morning Mama'd been at Lena's looking at wigs she had to special order. Mama has to act like she knows everything, even things she won't there for.

Daddy looks at Wayne and says they'll have to take care of the bear, because ol' Hiram sure can't. "Better do it 'fore dark," Mama says. "'Fore them dogs get to it." Mama's always complaining about the dogs ripping and rearing around Hiram's house. She says they're wild and they just turn up there because Hiram feeds them. She says he ought to know better than that.

Abner comes back to the table.

And Sister pours him more tea.

Daddy tells Mama that her wig looks nice. But he says "hair" instead of "wig."

Mama says Lena tried to convince her to get the one with the red wash on it. "But I don't need no wash at my age," she says. She fluffs her wig and laughs. "I'll look about like that cashier woman in Food Lion, hussy like."

Wayne and Daddy and Sister laugh a little at that.

There's three butterbeans left on Abner's plate and he's moving them around with his fingers. He looks at Sister and says, "Wash." He eats one butterbean at a time and says, "Wash on her hair, wash on the land, the world needs to be washed in the blood of the Lamb."

"Stop that messing, Abner," Mama says. "I don't know where you think you are eating with your hands like that at the table."

Daddy takes his cap off and pushes his hair off his forehead. It's sticky from sweat. He puts his hat back on, and lets it sit loose.

Abner starts singing, "*Are you washed...in the blood...in the snow cleansing blood of the lamb?*"

Sister looks at me like she's afraid. Abner's never sang at the table like this.

"That's right, Abner," Wayne says to him laughing, "like what we sing in church."

Abner nods his head and keeps going, "*Are your garments spotless, are they white as snow?*"

And I don't sing it out loud but I sing it in my head, I join in with Abner to finish it, "*Are you washed in the blood of the lamb?*"

And he gets up from the table. The table shakes again. Abner turns his glass up and gets whatever ice is left in it. He walks out, crunching it with his teeth.

"See y'all later," he says and he throws up a wave behind him.

"See you later, Abner," Daddy says as the door slams.

Everybody's through eating.

Daddy and Wayne head to the living room to take their naps during the stories. They can't be in the field in the middle of the day like this. "Daddy, y'all ought to go on out there now and tend to that bear," Mama yells from the kitchen. "'Fore it gets to smelling too bad, the heat like it is."

I get the scraps together to take out to the cats. Mama hands me some cantaloupe she can't finish. On the porch I can hear her telling Sister how to wash the plates.

I go out to the smokehouse and the cats come out from everywhere like they're starving. Running over each other, meowing. When they're eating like that is the only time you can touch them. They're real skittish. There's a little black one with a white spot on her chest. She's the runt. I've been trying to get her to like me and I think it's working 'cause when I touch her now when she's eating, she purrs. So before long I'll be able to get my hands on her and hold her soft under my neck.

Since we ain't had no rain, I've been giving the cats water plenty times a day. I keep one of the gallon buckets ice cream comes in at the back of the smokehouse in a shady spot for them. I grab the bucket and dump their old water out on Mama's hydrangeas and take the bucket to the pump. The sky is still heavy and the dirt under my feet is cool like it's gonna rain.

I look out towards that fallow field and see the vultures circling. I walk to the edge of the yard to get closer. That's when I see Abner out there. He's punching his arms up at them. He starts slinging hisself faster and harder. He's singing, "*What can wash away my sin?*" He's moving back and forth in front of the bear. It's laying there still, a big black shape. They're all out there far from me. They can't hear me but I come in with

Abner, singing loud as I can, "*Nothing but the blood of Jesus*!" Then Abner stops everything, kicks the bear in the face. And he stands there looking at it real still.

"C'mon in the house," I yell to him. Abner turns around and sees me looking at him. I watch him coming to me fast, holding out his arms.

And before I know it, Abner's holding me. I'm shaking.

"It's alright," he says. "It's alright."

Lorene

orene's mama found her out behind the barn, under the sweet Betsy bush. She was laying there with her eyes closed. It was May, a pretty afternoon, the sun was shining, and the birds were singing. But Lorene couldn't stop crying. She said she felt trapped and her mama didn't know what to do. The doctor in town said maybe a change of scenery would help her. This was 1958. Lorene was fifteen.

So, she went to live with her sister, Jane Ann, in Rocky Mount. Jane Ann was a seamstress and married to Billy, a photographer for the paper there. They had two children, Baby Barbara and Tom. It was nice in Rocky Mount, the trains were always running. And Lorene could walk to the library, check out all the books she wanted about Mexico.

Lorene was shy. She didn't talk much. She wasn't close with her sister or brother-in-law, Baby Barbara or Tom. And she still cried from time to time. But at least she won't on the farm anymore still having to use an outhouse, waking to miles and miles of fields and nothing.

In Rocky Mount all she had to do was help with the children and wonder if the kids at her new school would like her blouses. She shared a bedroom with Tom. She hung out the laundry, gave Baby Barbara the bottle and dusted every week. She read about Mayans and Incas and Aztecs. She looked at pictures of The Goddess of the Dead drawn on walls and pots and jewelry—her mouth was always open, she ate the morning stars.

And then one night at supper there was a moth fluttering at the screen door trying to get in. And Lorene felt she was the only one who saw it. So she got up from the dinner table and stood at the screen and pressed her face where it was fluttering on the other side. She wanted to feel how soft its wings were, like powder on her cheeks.

But Jane Ann called her back to the table.

And then that's when Billy said it. "Lorene you've got quite the eye—quite the eye for detail," he said.

Lorene blushed.

Billy was eating a chicken leg clean.

She sat down and looked at her lap. "I'm sorry," she said. "I just wanted to see it real close."

Jane Ann was holding Baby Barbara. She was gnawing on her hands.

Then Tom piped up. "We've got to catch it," he said. He

slammed his hand flat on the table. Everyone ignored him, but the ice in Lorene's tea clinked.

"Ain't your birthday coming up soon?" Billy said.

Lorene could feel him looking at her. It felt like a bolt of lightning.

"Yes," she said into her lap. "In a couple of days. August 20th."

Billy was tearing up his roll, sopping up the last of his sweet corn juice. "Well, we'll have to do something," he said.

Jane Ann sucked in real quick then, Baby Barbara had bit her with growing teeth.

When it came time for Lorene's birthday, Billy gave her a camera. And she brought it with her everywhere. She saw how in the late afternoons the camellias hung with heavy blossoms and the holly bush reached through the fence.

And then, during the night, Billy started slipping notes under her bedroom door, with instructions on how to capture light. Then close-ups. Then texture. Then "I always think of you."

So, when he asked Lorene to run away with him, she did it gladly.

She dreamed of Jane Ann re-marrying a mailman with a small belly, one who'd make the children pancakes from scratch. She dreamed of visiting temples and mountains on assignment for *National Geographic* and *Time*.

But what happened was Billy took her to Acapulco and strangled her with beautiful silk scarves. She gasped and gasped into the morning. She lost her virginity and took care of what would have been the baby. And then Billy left her too.

But Lorene kept the camera he gave her, it sits on the shelf. She's a cleaning lady at a hotel now. She's shy and doesn't talk much. She walks on the beach at night, pretends she sees dolphins. And sometimes, while washing mirrors, she looks at herself and opens her mouth.

Jacuzzi

The first time I went to Myrtle Beach was with Courtney Robbins. She told me to roll up my shorts to show off my legs. She wore a string bikini. She wanted us to get boyfriends. We rode the elevators at night and stopped on every floor to see who'd get on. Her mama drank in the hotel bar with her boyfriend.

We went to the Ripley's Believe It or Not aquarium and took pictures in the shark tunnel. We got puka shell necklaces from the gift shop. We ate Sour Cream & Onion Pringles. We walked up and down the beach pulling gummy worms out our mouths until they dissolved on our tongues. We got tans. And then two boys were behind us in the snow cone line. And then Courtney went to singing that To The Window To The Wall Till The Sweat Drop Down My Balls All These Bitches Crawl song which made me blush but she elbowed me to join in. She knew I didn't like that music. She knew I'd never had a boyfriend. She knew I'd never been kissed.

She didn't have a daddy. She could probably count on one hand how many times she'd ever seen him. She slept with a pee pad on her bed. Her house was outside of town, across the railroad tracks. She stuffed her bra with toilet paper. Sometimes, when we slept together, I woke up with her holding my hand.

The boys in the snow cone line asked us where we were from and of course they'd never heard of it, but we'd never heard of where they were from either. But we were all staying in the same hotel so we decided we'd meet up with them in the jacuzzi later. They wore caps and silver chain necklaces. They said they were twelve, thirteen and they'd be leaving on Sunday. "Us too," Courtney said.

Courtney was skinnier than me in every way but somehow her boobs were bigger and that made me feel dumb. But it was exciting when the boys showed up. I told them I'd never been in a jacuzzi before. And they said they hadn't either. But Courtney did what she always did to try and look cool and lied. She said her daddy had a jacuzzi and she'd been in it plenty of times.

It was hot and my seat was gritty with sand. Courtney scooched over to the boy with freckles. I watched the bubbles keep coming and asked them all if they thought it'd be okay if I put my head underwater. No one got kisses that night, or touches, we just went back home more tanned. But Courtney told everybody at school that me and her got drunk at Myrtle

Beach. She said we made out and did other stuff she couldn't remember. Davis Askew turned around and licked his lips at me in the auditorium. I didn't like it. And I didn't talk to Courtney anymore after that.

Sleepovers

Nicki chewed on pen caps and twisted them with her teeth. She tore off pieces and kept them in her mouth. You could see them sitting on her tongue when she talked. I could never figure how she did that without choking.

She came into our class in the fourth grade. She'd just had her appendix taken out and the boys picked on her. Will Fletcher said she smelled like pigs. Her daddy was a hog farmer. His hog houses were back off the road on the way to school. Sometimes on the playground, when the wind blew right on the top of the swings, you could smell them.

Nicki and her family had moved down from Virginia. She had three sisters and they all had lots of freckles and long blonde hair.

I'd never seen hair so thick and frizzy before. They all wore worn-out clothes that looked like mine just faded. And they all lived with their mama and daddy in front of their hog houses way back off road on the way to school. You could see their trailer sitting back there every morning. It was yellow down a long dirt path.

And Nicki had a lisp—I'd never heard anybody talk like that. She was the littlest girl in our class. She sat in front of me and her shoulder bones stuck outta her sleeveless tops. She was the second oldest sister.

When they had sleepovers it was like all the girls at school got invited. We played hide-and-go-seek and three girls would squish together in the same spot. One time I got a spot to myself in the kitchen cabinet and I saw a mouse caught in a trap. I screamed then we all screamed and then Nicki's sister Samantha came in there and told us to shut up or we'd wake up their mama and daddy. Samantha was the oldest and we all huddled together hanging outside the storm door to watch her fling that mouse off the porch. It was flying in the air when Nicki said "Look—it's still wiggling." It's little body shined in the porch light or maybe it was moonlight before it disappeared in the yard. "Poor thing," Samantha said. "It's half dead, half alive."

Samantha always did our makeovers. I loved her to French-braid my hair. She never pulled it too tight. And to make things work good with so many girls, Samantha made a rule that when she was braiding somebody's hair, that girl would be brushing somebody else's hair and getting her ready.

At the first sleepover, Nicki asked me to brush her hair. I remember thinking that I didn't want to hurt her. There was probably lots of tangles in her thick thick frizzy hair, maybe in the little baby hairs up around her neck. But I got all her hair in my hands and smoothed it down her back. Then I started brushing from the bottom, working out the knots. And then once all the knots were gone, I took the brush and ran it down from the top of her head all the way to the bottom. I remember she shook like she had goosebumps then, turned around and giggled, "You're giving me the tinglys."

Samantha told us to hold our breath when she put her mama's nice Mary Kay mascara on us that way we wouldn't blink. And she told us how the lipstick and eyeshadow she gave us went with our season and what that all meant. And she had a special hand mirror with sparkles in it that she used to show us our new look. And then she'd make all the girls who were too scared to get makeovers get up off the living room floor where they were giggling and carrying on, they'd move their sleeping bags out the way, clear us a circle, and we'd walk around it so everyone could see our new look.

And then we'd lay down, so many of us all together. You had to tiptoe not to step on anybody. And we'd watch *Titanic* and look at Rose's naked body on that fancy couch, her pretty breasts heaving under that big necklace. As soon as it was over the Barrett Twins would holler for somebody to rewind it. And we'd watch it again and again—"the naked part."

In the fall, Nicki's daddy got his leg tore off in one of the hog houses. He got caught in a piece of equipment. Every time anybody talked about it all I could think of was how he'd wallowed in pig shit and slosh after his leg had been ripped off, dragging himself through all that mess to get some help, with all the pigs grunting and running around, slick and mud wet.

The school threw a spaghetti supper for him. To raise money so he could get a fake leg. But when he got it, it won't quite right. Like it was too little or something and he hobbled around the best he could at basketball games. And then everyone would go to him on the bottom bleacher and shake his hand and tell him how pretty all his girls were.

Everyone put Nicki's daddy on the prayer list. And Mama gave me black trash bags and told me to put clothes in them I didn't want nomore. She said she was gonna take them to Nicki and her sisters. I filled the bags but didn't go with her. Mama came back and talked all night at supper how Nicki and her sisters smiled when they saw all the clothes, how they started trying them on right there in the middle of the living room floor.

At the lunch table the girls talked about Nicki's new dress, how they thought she looked nicer. It was black and white plaid with yellow sunflower buttons. I didn't tell them it used to be mine. In class I thought about her shoulder bones, were they sticking out more? And I wanted to brush her hair. She turned around and asked me if she could please borrow a pen. Will Fletcher looked at me and said, "She's gonna eat it." I reached into my pencil box and grabbed a pen that I had chewed on and gave it to her. She took it and started to trace a picture of one of them wild horses running on the beach. She really liked that section in our North Carolina notebook, how those horses swam to shore after shipwrecks and stayed there in their own horse families, taking care of each other for hundreds of years in their own horse way. I watched Nicki work on the wild horses. She'd scratch out the tail and start again to get it right.

The next thing we knew all the sisters stopped coming to school one day. The teacher told us they'd gone back to Virginia. We emptied Nicki's desk out. The boys tipped it over and all her wadded up homework and half used notebooks spilled out.

Us girls dumped out her pencil box. She didn't really have any crayon colors we needed. She didn't really have many crayons at all. All she had was the regular colors that everybody has, nothing special. But we split them between us anyways. And I stayed and dug for a pen cap to keep.

Return to the Coondog Castle

Cricket rode by where her husband is living with that Coonie girl, in that little shack house behind the black Baptist church. And she saw that girl sitting out there on the front porch and Cricket couldn't help but feel sorry for her and hate her at the same time. The girl was spinning around in a computer chair, holding her legs out in front of her in the air. She'd put her legs down, stop herself quick and then push her feet on the porch floor, propelling herself again.

And now this is the first time Cricket's seen her husband since she threw him out. That was eight months ago, when she found out he'd been sleeping with Coonie's daughter. She told everybody she threw him out because of the drugs. And that was half the truth. He'd been doing good for their three years of marriage and then he started back using. But everybody knows Daniel Adam has always been getting into trouble with meth. And "drugs" is easier to say than "infidelity" or "affair."

Last night Cricket held up her family's old christening gown, the one she'd worn and everyone before her had worn too. She held it in front of her and thought there wasn't a need for her to have it. And she cried not so much because her husband didn't think of her, but because she was farther away from the family that they could have had.

Cricket's mama always told her that respect and communication and honesty were what kept her and Cricket's daddy together all those years. Her mama tells Cricket not to blame herself. But also, "You can do better," and, "You've got time."

But her mama does not know how she feels watching Daniel Adam coming up her front steps. He's got her Bible in his hands, the one with Cricket's name in the corner with golden shiny letters, the first Bible she ever got, the one she'd left in the side door of Daniel Adam's truck, the one she thought about before she prayed at night, hoping that girl would see it. Cricket figured if that girl had a conscience she'd feel bad looking at it and maybe it would make her stop and realize what all she was doing. That girl would stop and tell Daniel Adam to go back home.

When Honey was a newborn pup the big storm flooded everything out. That was last fall when all the chickens drowned and kept turning up in the woods and the swamp and in the ditches in town. Honey and her family were brought in the big people house because their dog house fell down when the big trees fell on it.

The house had lots of things in it, things in the way. And it felt funny under their feet. And the smells of all the chickens outside made them want to run circles around and around inside all day long. They could hear the stray dogs and cats and birds digging in their teeth and claws and talons and pulling apart what they wanted to get into so bad. That wasn't fair to Honey and her family. But they were dogs and they were trained to listen to rules. They were trained to hunt coons, and they were really good at it, so good that people from far away came to take them even farther away to places with names they'd never heard of to hunt coons on new lands. So when the Man said in a low, strong voice, "No," they knew "Bad" and they didn't run around the house. Only outside for bathroom and play.

But Honey had it the best because she was the Girl's favorite. Honey doesn't remember, but the Girl was there to help pull her into the world when her mama was pushing her out.

Right now Honey is burrowing herself into the roots of a very old and big tree. It's the middle-of-the-day-hot and the dirt there is cool and it feels nice. She lays down and remembers being in the Girl's bed. How she wanted to be so close to the Girl, underneath and between her legs. The Girl's ankles smelled extra nice sometimes before bed like sweet and Honey remembers licking them.

It was nice but crowded in the people house so it was good news when some men started making Honey and her family a new house out back. The Girl would hold Honey up in her bedroom window to look at the new dog house. The Girl pointed with her finger and Honey followed it to see one of the men, the one with the long string of hair down his back. That man told the Girl he was building Honey a castle. The Girl said Honey could sleep in her own tower. Honey didn't know the words "castle" or "tower" but the Girl sounded excited and happy when she said them. The Girl scratched behind Honey's ears extra then, whenever she talked about that man.

Then one day the Man with the rules left and the men stopped building the castle and the Girl told Honey goodbye. After all that, the woman in the people house made Honey and her family stay in the castle. It was different than their house before. It was taller and there was steps inside like the big people house. The steps went up to a little room with a window. From the window Honey could see way behind the castle, to the edge of the field. Honey liked to look there in the morning when the clouds were on the ground, to see if she could see any deer, bringing their heads up to listen around them while they ate peanuts. And even though Honey liked that spot in the castle, there were other parts that were not good. Some parts had holes and rain came in and made mud on the ground and the woman yelled when they rolled in it. And some walls had sharp long teeth-like things that stuck out of them and Honey's family got caught on them and bled. The castle was not good. Honey missed the Girl so one day she ran out the castle and towards the deer. It felt good to run as hard as she could, chasing the deer far into the woods. Since living alone in the woods behind the castle, Honey has killed three coons and seven squirrels. And she rests here in the cool dirt, between the roots of the big old tree, thinking about the Girl until she smells what it is she's going to chase after next.

Megan's been waiting at the house all day thinking about Daniel Adam's body, how he makes her feel full when he's inside her, and what he says, "I want to make you feel good all the time." But he's late coming home. He said he'd be right on. He said he'd bring her Mango Smirnoff to drink because today is her birthday—she's seventeen.

So she's been thinking about Daniel Adam's body. And she's been thinking about how she's gonna tell him his baby is inside her. She's not showing yet but she knows it's there. She feels it slosh in her belly when she spins in her computer chair. She's afraid of what will happen.

The first time Daniel Adam touched her was when Megan's daddy gave her some money and told her to ride with him to the Duck Thru to pick up some hotdogs for everybody working on the coon castle back at the house. When they got out of the truck, Daniel Adam took Megan's hand and led her behind the Duck Thru till she was back against the wall. She had never been kissed and he grabbed her by the jaw and opened her mouth with his. She pushed herself up on her tiptoes. She kissed him back and pulled him down to her, his body pressing her into the wall. She bit him and she felt herself get very wet in her panties. She'd never felt that before. He bit her back. Then she opened her eyes and he was looking right at her. She bit even harder and drew his blood. He wiped his mouth and she saw the white chickens floating down behind him in the ditch, going under the road.

"Your eyes get big like an animal when you're biting me, girl," he said. "Who taught you that?"

And again, "Who taught you that?" when she pulled his rattail so tight between her toes that he couldn't move his head, only put his fingers fast inside her so she saw stars spinning from far away like how God saw them during creation. And then over and over, during all this time, "I've been planning on leaving my wife."

Megan's sitting here in her computer chair, sprawling out her legs, smelling her sweat smells, waiting for something to happen. Daniel Adam's still married. He could be anywhere he wanted in that truck. He could be looking Cricket right into that one eye of hers that has the double pupil, that eye he wakes up in the middle of the night thinking about. Scribbling in his notebook, saying, "Go back to sleep, I'm just drawing a closet." Not letting Megan see what he's doing. Saying he's busting bottles out front in the yard to help his hurting. Out there saying he loves his wife. Getting fucked up, coming back in to her.

One time he handed Megan a knife in the kitchen. "Cut me, I know you want to," he said. He was on his knees then on the floor.

All the notes Daniel Adam leaves for her to find in the house when he leaves in the morning. "You're beautiful" on the ice pops in the freezer. "Big booty smack" on the toilet. "Sexy" on the ceiling fan. Daniel Adam could have done and said all these things with Cricket before. And Megan feels dumb and stupid, and sometimes she tells herself she is dumb and stupid. But one thing Megan can do is check on her tomatoes. She gets up and goes to the garden, picks a cherry tomato and squeezes it between her thumb and pointer finger. She thinks about stripping Daniel Adam clear naked and cutting his head off with that bowie knife he keeps in his glovebox. Leaving his body down that McDaniel farm path where they found that old woman in the ditch. Since that old woman's spirit's already spooking the place, Daniel Adam won't be able to spook it. He don't deserve a place to linger around on. She thinks about holding his head by the rattail like when Deborah in the Bible held that one man's head who was so awful to her. Megan could hold him just right so she could look him straight in the eyes, not have to look up to him. She'd be able to see the moon and herself in them and she could swing his head around her head until she threw him into the growing cotton. Megan wants to pick him up by his rattail from that cotton and swing his head into some pines at the edge of the field like she's trying to beat the dirt out of a floor mat. Megan wants to put her feet on either side of the top of his head, pull up on his rattail for balance and bounce on his skull. She wants to feel her weight cracking him, his bone squishing into his brain. She won't feel the baby moving inside her then. Maybe it will even get still. The tomato bursts between Megan's fingers. She doesn't want to be a bad person. She hates Daniel Adam for making her a bad person.

Since the death of her husband Mrs. Creech has been eating mostly Special K for dinner, the kind with the red berries in it and sometimes J.J.'s carries it and sometimes they don't. But she always asks the Richards girl working the register anyways because there might be some in the back that they ain't put out yet, because that's happened before. So when Mrs. Creech comes in the door, that Richards girl goes to the back and today one box of Special K with the red berries is left in the whole store.

Mrs. Creech puts it on the grocery belt with milk, eggs, white bread, and baloney. When the Richards girl picks up the cereal box, Mrs. Creech tells her the doctor show on TV said that red berries help with your memory. Also deodorant without aluminum is what you're supposed to use and the only place to get that around here is Walgreens in Ahoskie, she's looked all over.

The Richards girl doesn't say much back, just bags the groceries. She's mighty shy and seems like she's in her own world and Mrs. Creech doesn't understand why J.J. would hire a girl like that to run the register. She don't even greet people when they come in the door. And that's important not only when running a business but in life. Mrs. Creech's mama raised her and her brothers and sisters to be able to talk to anybody, no matter what. "Nobody is ever so good or bad that you can't talk to them," she said.

Coonie's daughter pushes the door too hard and it flies open. She looks sweaty but still very pretty like she always has. She walks fast into the aisles. The whole town knows the story, how Daniel Adam's keeping her in that shack house behind the Black church. He's probably got her on drugs. Mrs. Creech has seen her out there tending the tomatoes. But here's the part only Mrs. Creech knows: Coonie's daughter coulda been with Daniel Adam the night he broke into her house, picking out all the jewelry she wanted from her jewelry box. The pieces her husband gave her over all the years: the bracelet with rubies on their first Christmas together in 1962, the ruby ring from the next Christmas to match it. It looked like a red little pinecone.

The Richards girl hands Mrs. Creech her change and asks her what kind of stone is in her ring. And Mrs. Creech felt herself falling into wanting to tell the girl all about it, how it keeps coming up. The love of her life is dead. She won't open his closet. She won't sleep in their room. How she still wakes up in the middle of the night on the couch in the living room where his hospice bed was. She wakes up to check on him, to make sure he's still breathing, to drop water in his mouth with a straw. To lightly scratch his back. But he's not there when she wakes. And this is heavy.

And she also wants to tell how during her husband's final hours when he had to be taken to die in the hospital, their home was broken into by Daniel Adam. Her husband had always gotten him to do their carpentry work, no matter how often Daniel Adam found himself on the wrong side of the tracks. And it was Daniel Adam, the one her husband always gave a second chance to who broke in when he knew her husband was dying, walked right past the living room where he'd been to see her husband down in his deathbed, telling him goodbye. Daniel Adam went straight to the secret jewelry cabinet he'd built for her in the dress closet. He took all the jewelry. He strew all the family photos on all the bedroom floors, clothes were thrown everywhere in the side yard. He took all the guns. He tried to take out the air conditioners.

And Mrs. Creech took her husband's hand and told him that the family home he so wanted to die in, where he'd been born upstairs, where he'd been talking to his dead sisters in the walls in and out of consciousness, was just fine, was just like he'd left it. Mrs. Creech lied to her husband because he was the best man she ever knew.

Daniel Adam's daddy was even a pallbearer for her husband. And this is a heaviness that also breaks Mrs. Creech in two. The detective couldn't find fingerprints. And nothing's turning up in the pawn shops around. Living in the country, the law isn't paid enough to really care for everyone. And now their oldest son, who was already fragile is in the middle of a nervous breakdown, has already tried to swallow rat poisoning. He won't leave his trailer except to ride to the Duck Thru for a drink.

And Mrs. Creech can't talk to her best friend, her husband, about any of it. He can't give her one guiding word. One of the last things he said to her was, "I'm glad it's me going before you because I know you can keep on living and I can't say the same for me."

So Mrs. Creech just holds herself back now in the J.J.'s checkout line. She does not want to worry the Richards girl with anything like this. So she tells the Richards girl she can't remember the name of the stone in her ring, "But my sister gave it to me. I don't really have any jewelry left, you know, from where they broke into my house."

She puts her change in her purse and hears the Richards girl say she's sorry. But how pretty the ring is, how she's never seen a stone like that before. Mrs. Creech thanks her and slowly grabs her bag.

Coonie's daughter comes up behind her in line with a box of macaroni and milk. She puts them down and starts to tighten her ponytail.

"I'm sorry," the Richards girl tells Coonie's daughter. "But Daniel Adam ain't paid his credit yet and you ain't supposed to get nothing till he pays."

"Well I got $2 right here," Coonie's daughter says handing her the money. "Please can you just let me get this today? I'm telling ya, Amy, this is what I want for supper—it's my birthday."

Mrs. Creech can tell by looking at her that Coonie's daughter walked here. Mrs. Creech can tell that girl is hungry for lots of things. Mrs. Creech wants to hug the girl, tell her happy birthday.

"Look here," Mrs. Creech turns to Coonie's daughter. "Now you keep your money and let me pay for it."

Coonie's daughter looks at Mrs. Creech with hurt animal eyes. She quickly grabs the box of macaroni and milk and says, "Thank you so much, thank you so much," as she runs out the door.

And Mrs. Creech will wait. She'll call her oldest son over from his trailer across the road and make him a baloney sandwich. She won't let him leave until she sees him swallow his anti-depressants. She'll pat him on the back and tell him goodnight. She'll wipe down the dinner table and then she'll finally sit. And that is where she'll cry.

On the way to church, the sisters pass the little patch of woods where Annie Pearl's too-early babies are buried. Annie Pearl always looks their way, sometimes says how sweet they were to hold, but that's it. Hildy's never talked about it with her sister, but she knows being a mama would have been the greatest joy of Annie Pearl's life. Hildy doesn't understand why God didn't let her sister be a mama.

When the sisters pull up at church they see that white girl upset and throwing bottles. She's busting them on the front steps of the shack house. She's crying, wiping her face and nose with the back of her hand. They sit in the car a minute and watch her.

"Drugs," Hildy says. "I'm telling you, that boy is in them drugs bad."

"Look at her though, something's going on. She ain't even seen we've pulled up." Annie Pearl shakes her head.

"Sister, we ain't gonna mess with it." Hildy pulls down her visor and straightens her hairpiece.

"He coulda hurt her, beat on her. He looks mean as a snake every time I've seen him."

"Now what you gonna do? You go over there and he's gonna beat on you too? Look, you do what you want, I'm going to decorate. I don't want nothing to do with it. We signed up to decorate for revival tonight and you know me, if I've got anything to do with it I'm gonna make sure it's perfect and I spent all week looking this flower chain to drape over the pulpit with them purple flowers like I want..."

Annie Pearl squints to look at the girl harder.

"I'm sure that girl is fine, Sister, maybe they're just in a spat." Hildy opens her car door. "Let's just wait and see if she's still out there after revival. And if she is, we'll go see about it."

Hildy leaves Annie Pearl sitting there pushing her glasses up on her face. She opens the boot and pulls out the flower chain. She hears the car door slam and looks and sees Annie Pearl making her way across the yard. The girl is really slinging a fit now.

Hildy can't hear what her sister is saying to the girl but the girl's moving her hands in the air, telling her sister something.

Annie Pearl is shaking her head in a gentle way.

It takes a minute but the closer Annie Pearl gets to the girl, the more the girl starts to calm down. She drops the bottles in her hands, stops pacing. Annie Pearl puts her arms around the girl and pats the back of her head. Hildy watches them and she thinks of the doll babies lined up on her sister's couch in new pink dresses.

Hildy looks back at the church, no one's showing up yet but the automatic lights in the flower beds have already come on. She looks back to Annie Pearl and the girl. The girl is much taller than Annie Pearl and she's got her arm over Annie Pearl's shoulder. The girl leans and puts her head on top of Annie Pearl's. Then Annie Pearl hollers across the yard for Hildy to call Erma to come and decorate, that they've got to help this girl.

Hildy glances in her rearview mirror and sees her sister wiping the girl's face with one hand and patting the girl's leg with the other. The girl is still crying but not as much.

"Does she need to go to the hospital, Sister?" Hildy asks.

"No," the girl says. "I just want to go home." And the girl sobs into Annie Pearl's chest.

"She's okay, Sister," Annie Pearl says, stroking the girl's wild hair. "Let's just get her to her mama. She needs her mama now."

"Take me to the coondog castle," the girl says. "Please."

"They didn't ever finish that did they?" Hildy says as she pulls out the drive.

"No." The girl looks into her lap.

"That's a shame," Hildy goes on. "That coulda been an attraction for the area. I bet folks woulda drove down from Virginia to see that."

"I know," the girl tilts her head. "Too bad my daddy had to screw everything up."

Annie Pearl hands the girl some tissue from her purse.

The girl blows her nose and gets quiet. Then she says, "Look you can just go on and tell her everything. I know she wants to know what's going on." The girl turns to Annie Pearl, "I don't care, tell her everything. I can feel her looking at me and thinking I'm crazy, but I'm not crazy! I'm just feeling like I—," the girl lifts her head like she's looking out beyond the top of the car. "I don't have no control over nothing. No control...I, I, I," she brings her head back down and starts to twist her hands in front of her, "I found her Bible in the truck door. Made me sick. I told him I didn't want to see it no more. And then he didn't come home. He don't love me. He don't love me! And I ain't got nothing! I ain't got..."

Annie Pearl pulls the girl closer and tells her it's alright.

Hildy stops looking at the girl. It's dark now. She takes a left at the light on Main Street. Most everything is abandoned and no one is out. Folks are home, some windows shine but it's so dark.

"Well baby, you didn't tell my sister the GOOD news," Annie Pearl says from behind.

Hildy sees Annie Pearl put her hand under the girl's chin. She lifts the girl's head. Hildy can see the girl's face is sad.

"Hildy, we've got a real miracle back here," Annie Pearl pauses and puts both her hands on the girl's shoulders. "Megan is going to have a baby. Ain't that a blessing?"

Megan bends over trying to catch her breath. She starts shaking.

"Oh baby, sweet baby," Annie Pearl says leaning over her.

"Well congratulations," Hildy says. She does not look back anymore, just watches the road as they drive on to the edge of town.

Hildy hears that Megan has almost stopped crying. She listens to Annie Pearl talk to her so calmly. It's so low she can't make anything out. And Hildy remembers something their mama'd say every time Annie Pearl was newly pregnant, "Eating summer corn brings sunshine to a baby in the belly."

"You know, I've got some fresh corn I've just blanched and canned in the boot," Hildy says.

"Yes baby, we'll give you some. It'll be good for you and that baby. It'll make y'all strong," Annie Pearl says.

Hildy looks and sees her sister smiling and she smiles back at her. Hildy hears her sister talking quietly again. She thinks she's talking to the baby. She's telling it a prayer.

What would you have done when your husband, the biggest Bluetick coonhound breeder this side of the river, was busted in

Big Bay Odom's dope ring out of Arrowhead trailer park, when you never even knew he had anything to do with it and he was thrown in prison and left you with all those dogs to care for that no one wants to buy anymore because your husband's a criminal and then you found your only child, your 16-year-old daughter, out in the dog house naked on top of a full grown married man who everybody knows steals when he owes drug money?

You'd carry on and do the best you could and try to get your daughter to stop messing with that man. That's what Janet wants everyone around here to know. She didn't throw Megan out. She didn't want her to end up dropping out of school, hanging on the porch of that shack house for everyone to ride by and see. She tried her best. Janet tried to tell Megan that Daniel Adam didn't really love her. But Megan wouldn't listen. And Megan ran away and refused to come back. She said she needed to be where she felt loved and that wasn't with her mama.

Now everyone looks at Janet, asks how she's doing, has put her on their prayer lists. She is living in a broken home. With a damn half-built giant dog house Coonie always dreamed of, driving two hours on weekends to see him for a few minutes. And when he asks if Megan's doing ok, if she's still catching for the softball team, Janet says, "Yes."

Right now she is looking at their marriage photo that Megan loved so much. When Megan found it in the attic she made a big deal about it. How could her mama and daddy ever looked that young and happy before? Megan made a special frame for it, spray-painted some sticks and wove them together. She hung it above her dresser, showed it to her friends when they came over for sleepovers. "Look at mama's hair!" she'd say and they'd all laugh.

Janet pulls it from the wall. She's done all she needed to do for the day. Fed the dogs, gave medicine to the ones that needed it, she forgot to take the clothes off the line but that could wait till tomorrow. She's tired and it's dark out. She lays down in Megan's bed with her wedding picture. She looks at it again before putting it on the nightstand. She wishes that for her daughter's birthday today, wherever Megan is, she will not be afraid. That is all she can hope for. And Janet goes to sleep to the sound of the dogs barking outside. It's nothing. Those dogs bark all the time now that everyone is gone.

The baby can hear. Mama is calling. She says, "Honey." There is nothing coming back to Mama except barks. She calls louder. The baby feels Mama running fast for a long time, and Mama keeps calling, and the barks turn to howls that get quieter and quieter and the baby can remember too, hearing someone say it was a blessing.

You Go Into the ABC Store and the Saleslady Says

Now you listen.

Do you believe in ghosts?

Because I'mma tell you right now they exist.

There's this one in my house, see, and I don't know what it's for. I hear it coming down the hall at night creaking the floor. Coming closer, closer. Until it gets to my bedroom. I can feel it looking at me, standing at the end of my bed, it feels like forever and I can't move. It comes and sits on my feet. So cold so heavy, like it's trying to push me down through the floor, under the house. And I stay there with the blanket over my head. I don't want to look at it.

They say the devil comes for you when you're weak. And Lord I know it. And Lord I'm angry— been left here so alone. All this hurt in my heart, what's happened to me.

And you know some of it. Everybody knows some of it. How my girls don't come home nomore. It's easy to figure. It's hard for them now, coming home to me. Their Daddy in the nursing home losing his mind, his memory. I tell them to come on home NOW, he MIGHT be able to still say their names.

And everybody wants to know. Asks me all the time when's the last time I saw my husband. Like I just threw him in the home whenever he started getting too bad for me to take care of by myself. Like I'm just getting on and dancing on bars and having men over to my house. Let me tell you, yesterday I sat and rubbed his hand for thirty minutes before he looked at me. I was calling him Baby like I always called him. I told him about our girls. I just went on and on. And he didn't say nothing.

He is a baby now, so afraid. You got to hold his hand and pull him out of bed, pull him to the table.

He's not my husband. I don't know where my husband is.

I want to believe he's the ghost that's been coming to me. If I could only pull back the covers and look, it might really be him trying to come see me, trying to pull me out of bed, twirl me on the floor. Spinning like we used to dance by the river. We met in the summer. I was wearing a blue dress. He loved to tell that story.

Could you look?

Could you pull back the covers and look?

'Cause what if it ain't him.

My husband. He's a ghost, a spirit, he's off somewhere else fishing, he's a fish going upstream, laying under a fallen tree, he's a baby that's too big for me to hold. I want to cradle him, with his clean hands.

Yesterday I watched him eat with his fingers. He dipped his roll in his sweet tea. He never liked sweet tea before.

Whoever he is, whatever he's becoming, he's got clean hands.

You remember how dirty they always were. Always working. Always grease and dirt way down beneath the fingernail. He fixed your carburetor, your cotton picker, your air conditioner. He built your girls a tree house. He BBQ'd a pig when your son got engaged. He gutted all the fish and he gave all the fish to all our neighbors. We all remember his hands.

Do you feel sad now? See I didn't mean to make you feel sad. But I got to get it out of me somehow I can feel it welling up inside when I just sit and think. Nobody to talk to. I'm alone in my house. Alone here. Preacher says I need to start writing and I've been working on a poem here's how it starts:

> I want to share my life with you, just another day
> But you're forgetting who I am
> As you fade away

See, you ask me how I am and here I am telling you. I'm telling you that sometimes I sit here at this counter and get so sad that I'm just staring. Just like my husband. Just nothing. I feel like I'm becoming nothing. I'm not his wife no more, I'm not his mama. My girls won't come home. I'm lost.

And then I hear her singing. Miss Ann Ruby. I can see her out behind you now. She's down in the ditch with her red pea coat. She's picking up trash. She's singing *What a friend we have in Jesus.*

Hear her?

I can hear her right now.

All our sins and griefs to bear, what a privilege to carry everything to God in prayer. Seems like she's out there every other morning, as old as she is. Cleaning out the ditch and talking to folks before they come in here. And yes I've called her nephew to come and pick her up and take her to the house. And I've seen him come out here and try to get her in the car and she fights him and screams at him. Folks think Miss Ann Ruby's crazy but I'll tell ya. She's lived with ghosts. Still living with them now. She knows 'em better than any of us.

See when I was little she lived by my school. She'd come in with that red peacoat, holding her guitar, and interrupt the teacher and ask us if we knew Jesus, that Jesus was our only friend. And the teacher would let her interrupt. Talk for as long as she wanted. She'd say, "Raise your hand if you love music." And we all would raise our hands. She'd say, "Raise your hands if you want to learn how to play it." And Cindy Liverman was the only one to keep her hand up and Miss Ann Ruby walked to her in her desk and stood over her and told her that God was going to touch her that night. God was proud she was going to learn how to play His music with Miss Ann Ruby. And at the end of it, the teacher just said thank you Miss Ann Ruby. And Miss Ann Ruby went on to the next classroom and did the same thing all over again.

And here's the other part you might not know, folks don't like to talk about it. For when she was a young mother—Miss Ann Ruby was a beautiful woman, a classically trained musician— her husband tied her and their son up in their basement and shot himself in front of them. Made them watch it. But she went on and raised her son to play the piano the prettiest you've ever heard. And then he killed himself too.

And we all know what happened last year but I'll tell it again. When them neighbor boys of hers, 13, 15 years old came over to help her take the clothes off the line like they'd always done. Knocked her in the head with a pipe and 'bout beat her to death. Threw her in the boot of her car. Poured gasoline all on the outside of it and lit it on fire. She was in that car burning. But she pulled herself out.

Oh what peace we often forfeit, oh what needless pain we bear. All because we do not carry everything to God in prayer.

Miss Ann Ruby she was waiting for me outside one day. She looked me good in the face. I hadn't been that close to her since I was a real little girl. She said I looked familiar. She asked me where I was from. And then before I could say anything her face turned to look like an angel. And she said, "I remember you, I've known you all your life."

And she's out there now waiting for you.

It's alright if you're lost.

But know you're not a stranger.

The Mattress

Hope's sitting at work, her daddy's septic tank business. She's the secretary. She's looking at seafood recipes on the computer, a seafood pizza to spice things up. She read in *Cosmo* that you can do that. Changing things up in the kitchen can entice your man to change things up in the bedroom. Because food and sex are both natural desires, going all the way back to caveman times.

Hope's husband is named Dale.

Dale's trying to sell a BeautyRest ReCharge Extra Firm mattress to an elderly woman. Her name is Mrs. Creech. But the elderly woman is buying the mattress for her son. It's a bit confusing.

Dale's laying down beside Mrs. Creech on the mattress.

She's telling him, "Now my boy Bobby, he's fat, I mean real fat."

"Yes ma'am," he says, his eyes closed.

"Now these springs gotta support him." She goes on.

Dale thinks of *My 600 Pound Life*, and Mrs. Creech's son inside his house, trapped like a whale. Hope loves that show, she laughs at the sad people and their loved ones washing out their fat layers and folds.

Dale's phone goes off then, vibrates the bed.

But Mrs. Creech doesn't notice, she pokes her finger into the mattress.

Hope's texted him and she wants to know: SHRIMP or SALMON.

Hope's daddy's septic tank business is a mile outside of town, across from wheat fields, and beside Arrowhead trailer park. No one really comes in the septic tank business until around 3pm when the schoolbus lets off the kids at Arrowhead. They buy Little Debbie cakes and Cokes and Snickers bars and Doritos that the septic tank business sells for snacks at the counter.

But right now it's noon and a girl Hope's seen before comes in with a baby on her hip and asks to use the phone. She says she needs to call her probation officer. And her phone's been cut off.

The baby is drooling and squirming. It reaches for Hope's hand when she pushes them the phone. It's wearing a tee shirt with a ladybug on it that says "Love bug."

The girl dials and says, "Yes ma'am," over and over.

Hope realizes then that the girl is Coonie's daughter. But she can't remember her name.

The baby squeals so the mama-girl puts it down. It crawls fast as lighting to the corner basket filled with dog toys.

Hope's two dachshunds, Pookie and Peanut, are currently at Puppy Paradise getting their nails painted: Strawberita and Lime.

The baby reaches for Pookie's favorite squeaky hamburger and Hope jumps up to snatch it from her.

Now the baby's screaming.

And the mama-girl hangs up the phone and grabs her, picks her up by the arm. "Shut up," she says. The baby wobbles standing on her own two legs and the girl whoops her. "Shut up," she says. She whoops her so hard the baby's knees buckle. And the baby is really squalling now.

Hope puts the hamburger toy in the dog basket.

The mama-girl picks up her baby and heads towards the door.

"Where are your yip dogs today," she asks her over the baby's cries.

Hope tells her they're just at the doggy salon.

"A doggy salon," the mama-girl pauses for a minute looking at the basket of toys. "Well I'll be," she says and walks out the door.

Hope sits behind her desk, reaches for a Snickers.

She still hears the baby squalling and Dale still hasn't answered her text.

Dale has always dreamed of taking Hope on an Alaskan cruise because she's always wanted to go since she was little. He dreams of making an Alaskan cruise baby. It would start with eskimo kisses, then he'd rub his nose down Hope's neck, 'round her arms and elbows, legs and butt too. And outside the porthole of their cabin, icebergs grow and somewhere, of course, cute polar bears cuddle under a blanket of snow.

But we return to him on the mattress with the elderly woman, Mrs. Creech.

"You know this is actually our bestselling mattress to bigger people," he says.

"You can call him fat," she says. "'Cause that's what he is, Bobby is sooo BIG. I'm telling ya."

Then she slaps the bed, "But you know what, I'll take it!"

This will be Dale's first sale in four days. He's been working alone all week. He's so excited. He tells the woman he'll deliver it too, no extra charge.

"Now, Bobby, my big son, he don't live with me," Mrs. Creech says. "I live in that big white farm house with the barn behind it out on 258. And Bobby, he lives across the road from me in that trailer. Can't hardly see it because of the pine trees. I told him we ought to cut them down when he put that trailer there. I told him that the pine cones were gonna tear his lawnmower all to pieces."

"I see," Dale says.

"But you go on and deliver it to him there in that trailer across from my house. I would get my other boy Craig to come get it but he can't leave the field cotton season like it is."

"I understand," Dale says.

"Thank you so much," Mrs. Creech reaches for Dale's hand. "That's so kind of you."

Dale's preparing the paperwork at his register for the BeautyRest ReCharge Extra Firm Mattress, when he sees a tall male figure walk in towards Mrs. Creech.

Dale hollers to him from the counter, welcomes him to the store.

"Oh, look here," Mrs. Creech says. "It's Craig! This here is my other boy! He ain't the fat one."

When Dale gets to them the man is pulling Mrs. Creech off the mattress. And she's telling him she's getting that special mattress. "Like the one you told me to get," she says.

Mrs. Creech looks at Dale with big eyes. "Show Craig the paperwork you got on it."

But the man doesn't take the paperwork from Dale's hand.

The man looks at Dale and mouths the word, "Sorry," and then ushers Mrs. Creech out of the store.

Dale watches them leave.

At the door he hears Mrs. Creech ask her son, "Are you sure, now? Are you sure he don't need it?"

For the seafood pizza, Hope will need to drive to Roanoke Rapids. That's where the Super Walmart is and they've got the good seafood and to get there you pass the sex store and she's never been but she always looks when she drives by. And the walls inside are bubblegum pink, the lights are neon yellow.

She's never had an orgasm but she's read about them, of course. She's Google-searching strap-on images. There are rubber penises and even glass. How would glass feel inside a warm body? Cool and then warmer, warmer?

She needs to know from Dale: SHRIMP or SALMON.

But this is what he texts her: WHICH WOULD YOU RATHER HAVE, BABY?

Hope knew it, Dale can never assert himself. She wants him to assert himself. Insert himself into her, plunging, thrusting hard. *Cosmo* says strap-ons allow you to show your man how you want it. SHOW YOUR MAN HOW YOU WANT IT.

She sighs. She doesn't even want seafood pizza anymore.

Hope's daddy walks in the office and she closes her search window. The desktop background is an aerial shot of Alaska. The sun is coming up over the mountains of snow.

Dale wants to see where he would have delivered the BeautyRest ReCharge Extra Firm mattress to Mrs. Creech's son. He drives out to the end of Highway 258 and sees Mrs. Creech's house just as she described it. The white house is big and glows amidst the dark fields around it. And the tin roof looks like a mirror under the moon. Only one light shines from the first floor. Maybe Mrs. Creech is watching TV.

Dale looks across the road for the trailer, but the yard is thick with pines and overgrown bushes. He pulls down the dirt path and makes his way to the back of the thicket. The grasses get taller and swish against his side windows. He keeps the headlights shining and even walks out into the grass and bushes, pulling back branches to see if anything's there.

Earth to Amy

Rami got killed the other night. He got shot down there at the stop sign at Aunt Nan's. He'd just closed his corner store in Aulander and was driving through. Three boys were down there waiting for him in the ditch. And they jumped up when he stopped at the stop sign and shot him to death right there. He didn't even have time to get to his gun. My cousin Craig's the one who found him. He heard the shots and went to see what was going on. Craig said Rami still had his seatbelt on, his foot on the brake pedal. His headlights were shining out into the corn. Those boys didn't get but two hundred dollars and his watch. They won't but eighteen.

◊ ◊ ◊

Seymour's sweeping in front of my register saying that people from where Rami's from don't believe in embalming the body. He's looking at me like he wants me to make a face. But I pretend I don't hear him.

The night Rami died folks came out from all over to leave him flowers and candles and signs outside his corner store. They held prayer circles out in the parking lot into the night.

Yesterday, one of the mamas of one of them boys was in here crying in the canned food aisle. She was talking to a woman she went to church with. She was saying she didn't raise her baby boy like that. She said the police came out to her house in the middle of the night and dragged him outta her arms like he was a criminal.

Last time I saw Rami, I bought a hotdog from him and he asked me how Russ was doing. And that meant a lot to me because nobody around here ever asks me about him because he's a married man. And a young girl like me shouldn't be wasting my time on him that's what my Aunt Nan said. You can just tell that's what people are thinking when I check them out in my line.

But Rami was different, seemed like he always saw the good in people. If you didn't have the money to pay him that day, he'd let you have it. And he was always taking care of stray cats at his store. From the time Russ moved down here he'd been trying to give him one. Rami told me that Russ needed a cat since he lived alone.

Russ moved down at the start of spring to work at that new coal ash pond they put in the county. He came from Ohio. That's where his wife and two little girls are. He never talks about them much but one time he told me that the baby girl cries when they gotta run the vacuum.

But this thing with Rami has really tore Russ all to pieces. He was worried it had something to do with him being Muslim, but really it just came down to the money. It's sad. He's been staying up all night reading anything he can find on the internet. We're supposed to go over tonight and bring Rami's wife and daughter some pizzas. But I haven't heard from Russ all day and this happens sometimes when he gets in his mind that he's ashamed of what me and him are doing.

I'm nineteen and I've got the young people arthritis in my fingers. I don't have a car and I live at home with my sister and Daddy. Our house is right down the road. Daddy used to be the postman before he got Alzheimer's and then he had to quit. He used to do taxidermy on the side too. He'd bring home the dead animals he'd pick up on his mail route and throw them in the freezer. We grew up in a home filled with taxidermy animals on the floors and walls and shelves. We had a rattlesnake behind the rocking chair, a beaver beside the TV, and a bobcat Daddy mounted above the couch. But we had to sell them as things got worse 'cause we needed the money. Everybody called Daddy "Pipeman."

When Daddy got sick, me and Sister had to find full time work best we could. She works the night shift at Pine Forest nursing home and stays with Daddy during the day. I watch him at night. Sister says we're gonna have to put him in a home soon. And I hate it but I know it's true. He can't hardly put a sentence together now. He goes through a lot of diapers.

Everybody around here knows Daddy because he used to

deliver their mail and after he first got sick, folks would come by and see him. But no one comes around anymore.

Seymour lets me leave early for my lunch break because it's so slow. "Tell Pipeman I said hello," he says. Like my Daddy knows who Seymour is more than a man on the moon.

I take the highway home, walk on the side of the road. It takes about six minutes. The heat makes my hair sweaty so I throw it up into a ponytail and convince myself that Russ is going to break up with me. I make a list in my head of my talents and what I have to offer and all I can come up with is I'm young and I don't have a fat belly like most girls around here and when I was little Daddy said I was his girl.

Before Daddy got sick, I worked with him out in his taxi-dermy shed. I'd sit up underneath him like a little puppy. I'd do whatever he told me. And one day he thought it would be cute if I'd make little outfits for this set of squirrels he had. I made a Cinderella and Snow White. I made an Amelia Earhart too. I took them and hid them in the back of the shed when Daddy was sick and we were selling all the other animals.

Russ ain't never seen them.

When I get in the house, my sister's on the couch, half-sleeping with bills on her chest. And Daddy's in the corner recliner, where he was when I left this morning. He's staring empty at the stories on TV. He don't look at me when I come in. He grits his teeth together like he's eating, it's a new thing he's started doing. He keeps doing this and staring at the TV when I bend over and give him a kiss.

I wake Sister up and tell her to go on and get in the shower if she wants to. She gets up and hands me the bills.

"We're behind by one-fifty on the electric," she says, yawning.

"What's new," I say.

She goes down the hall to the bathroom, I go to the kitchen and open the cabinet, grab a Cup O' Noodles for me and Daddy's lunch.

"We'll figure it out," I yell to her.

Daddy used to grow his own herbs out back and now I just bring the shakey kind home from work because me and Sister let the garden die. But Daddy don't know the difference. Like right now I'm cutting his noodles so he can eat them better. And I'm shaking some dried basil on top. And no matter what I do to these shit noodles, he's still gonna smack on them just the same after he gets them.

I wake him up and check to see if I need to change him. And he does need a changing but dammit I don't want to do it. Thank God it ain't shit. Sister's the one who knows how to do it right. I might hurt him. I'm scared I'll hurt him just pulling on him to get him to sit up straight in his recliner. But after I've been tugging on him a while, he finally looks at me and I smile at him. I bring him his bowl of noodles and feed him a couple of bites to get him going on his own.

I go to the kitchen to get my Cup O' Noodles when I hear him trying to say "Old, old" at the TV. *The Young and the Restless* is on and when I come back to the living room with my lunch I see Victor Newman up there.

"Yeah Daddy, he is old ain't he," I say and then the pain comes real fast in my fingers and I drop my Cup O'Noodles, looks like tapeworms digging into the carpet.

I clean it up but Daddy don't seem to notice. And I know it's bad but all I can think about then is what I'm gonna say at his funeral, how we're gonna pay for it.

When Daddy sees me on the floor in front of him he says just as clear as a bell, "You're my pretty girl."

It's a lot. Everything is a lot.

My phone dings. It's a text from Seymour: EARTH TO AMY. WHERE U AT?

Before I head back to work I go out in the shed and grab my old squirrels; Cinderella, Snow White, and Amelia Earhart. I carry them under my arms and start back on the side of the highway. It's still hot out but a car goes by and blows a breeze. I think about Rami's wife and daughter. The daughter's about my age. She goes to the community college. Bet they never thought they'd wake up one morning without a husband and a daddy. I bet Rami loved them more than anything in this world. When Daddy would tuck me and sister in at night he'd say, "I love y'all more than anything in this world."

My phone rings Russ's special ringer and I stand there on the side of the road and put my squirrels down gentle to see what he's got to say.

"I miss your mouth." That's the first thing he says.

I want to tell him I miss him. I want to tell him I love him. I want to tell him when he touches me he takes me out of here. But I don't say any of it.

I watch the dress I made Cinderella all those years ago sparkle in the sun. I made it out of my frilly blue baby socks.

And Russ goes on a rant about the boys who killed Rami. He says he hopes they get the death penalty, says he wants to blow their brains out. He asks me what kind of pizza we should get Rami's family.

And I tell him I don't know if there's certain things Muslims can't eat.

"Yeah, that's smart," he says.

We agree on cheese.

He says he'll place an order for them from the place in Potecasi and swing by and get me after work. And then he says after we visit Rami's family maybe we can go to Bull Hill. That's where he took my virginity. "Maybe we can play around in the truck bed," he says.

I'm looking at Snow White now and I'd forgotten until now, but I even made her a little apple out of an eraserhead.

"I've got to go," I say.

After we hang up, I pick up my squirrels again and brush the grass out their tails. I pass the house where the new puppy's always squealing, sounds like it's getting its ears pulled apart.

I walk in the store and tell Seymour that I need to sell my squirrels in here. I sit my squirrels behind my register and grab my stool. I tell him I can clear that shelf above the candy racks where he displays his Wild Turkey bottles. "They ain't nothing but decoration," I say.

He's smacking on a Fudge Round, leaning over my register, "I don't know what all goes on in that brain of yours Amy, but I like it."

I stand on the stool and start throwing him his Wild Turkey bottles.

And then I set up my squirrel girls while he stands underneath me, his mouth open. "Is that one that woman who crashed her plane in the ocean?" he's pointing at Amelia.

"No," I turn around and look down at him. "She's the first woman to fly solo across the Atlantic ocean." I hop down off my stool, "And see that airplane behind her?"

Seymour nods and tucks his shirt under his belly flap.

"I cut that out from the *National Geographic* at school."

The rest of the day, the regulars come in and Seymour hollers at them to look at my squirrels. "She thinks she's gonna make some money off of them," he laughs.

And everybody around here knows who I am and remembers my Daddy and when Seymour says this they glance up at my squirrels and turn to me with a half-smile, like they feel sorry for me. And that's not what I want. But Daddy always said, "You can't control other people."

Don't nobody really stop to look at them except Miss Janet and she's got her granddaughter with her and her granddaughter is pointing at Cinderella's crown. I remember making that with leftover Christmas tinsel. I made a mess of silver shreds on the floor but it made Daddy so happy to see me working so hard in the middle of it.

I tell Miss Janet I can take Cinderella down if her granddaughter wants a closer look. I come out from behind my register and ask the little girl if she wants to see her. But Miss Janet takes her granddaughter's hand and pulls her close to her. "It's alright, honey," she says to me. She looks me up and down. Her granddaughter is pointing up at my squirrel Cinderella, she's excited and trying to get out of her grandmama's hold. "I know your Daddy sure is proud of you," Miss Janet says with that half-smile again. Her granddaughter is yanking at her arm now.

"How is he doing anyways," she asks me. And I tell her, "About the same," like always. "Well I'm thinking about y'all," she says. This is what they all say. This is what they always say. Don't reach out to hug me or nothing.

Buttercup

Joanie had a cousin with braces and a cousin that was slow and those two cousins were sisters. And one time when I was at Joanie's house, those cousins came over because the one with the braces was going to prom and she wanted to show Joanie's family her dress. While the braces one twirled in the living room the slow one kept putting her arms into her shirt so she looked dismembered. But nobody seemed to pay attention to what she was doing except me. Her name was Tina.

Tina sometimes sat around and tried to see how long she could hold her breath, her cheeks puffed out like the marshmallow challenge. Her sister with braces was named Bri and she was going to the prom with the preacher's son who got paralyzed in a drunk driving accident. He was really handsome and it was really sad. All the daddies got together and built him a ramp so he could get into the high school building at school.

Joanie kept a picture of Bri and him from the prom in her bedroom. It was on the wall above her lava lamp and at nighttime when she turned it on and it got going, it would goo goo and reflect up on Bri sitting pretty on that preacher boy's lap, her braces shining. And her pretty pink prom dress glittering like a princess.

Joanie's favorite color was lime green and her mama let her paint her walls whatever she wanted. So they were lime green and then lime green with a hot pink accent wall. And then lime green with a hot pink accent wall with black stripes.

Joanie had a computer in her bedroom too and we'd play *The Sims* into the morning, taking turns updating our families. Her goal was to always make her husbands and wives have affairs. And she liked getting the ones with low cooking skills in the kitchen without a fire alarm so they'd catch on fire and die. Or put them in the pool and then take out the ladder so they'd swim to death. She thought it was funny.

My goal was to always have as many children as possible. My husband was Brandon Flowers of The Killers. When me and Mama went to CVS, I saw them in the *Rolling Stone* magazine and I read in there that he was Mormon so it all made sense to me to have as many children as possible with him on the Sims. Joanie didn't like the Killers, she liked 50 Cent. She didn't like to read like me either. But she was really good at basketball. She always scored when she shot. And the boys loved her and were sending her notes all the time.

Joanie only saw her real daddy on special occasions. He lived far away with his new family. I never saw him myself. Joanie lived with her mama and stepdaddy and half brother. He was a baby and it was fun to play with him and tote him around and give him piggyback rides. His breath always smelled like pickles.

Joanie's cousin who was a little slow named Tina had this blankie she carried around with her that was full of holes like she'd worn it slam out. And one time when her and her sister, Bri, came over, Joanie's mama got all of us girls out in the front yard to take some pictures in front of her azaleas because they were blooming so big and she was so proud of them. So it was me and Joanie and Bri and Tina and I was next to Tina and she kept stroking my arm up and down with that blankie while we were standing there trying to take that picture. "She likes you," Joanie said.

Nobody knows this but I sucked my thumb until I was in the third grade and that was something I was embarrassed about. I was also really bad at math and had to stay in and write my multiplication tables with the boys writing sentences for misbehaving, while everyone else was outside going down the big slide.

When we were out by the azaleas then I picked a buttercup from the yard and held it up under Tina's chin and when it reflected yellow on her skin, I told her she liked butter. She called me Buttercup after that. Yellow has always been my favorite color.

Joanie ended up having a baby and moving to Greenville to be a waitress. Bri did good and got her dental hygiene degree. She works in Dr. Outland's office, married a big farmer and don't want for nothing anymore. Only time I see Tina now is when Bri and her mama bring her into the café to eat on Sundays. She hugs my neck when she sees me and they put a bib on her like a baby. She's a full grown woman like me now.

The Country Woman

When the woman's ancient family died, she was left with their farm and farm house. She'd grown up there but left for college. In the city, she studied history, specifically Elizabethan, but more specifically, she went to parties and danced and twirled in the arms of anyone who would listen to her tell about where she was from. How she grew up without ever knowing a stranger. How she was related to everyone. How she dreamed of reading books about people she saw on PBS documentaries—she'd wake up in the middle of the night and come downstairs and sit in front of the TV, learning about worlds far from the cotton fields outside her window.

"Don't your parents read," everyone would ask her.

And she'd laugh.

No one could believe it.

Of course she couldn't find a job in the city after graduating and there was only so much galavanting to museums and symphonies left to do before, as mentioned earlier, all her family died and she had to come back home to her inherited destiny: the land.

The woman said goodbye to all her like-minded friends and cultural indulgences—goodbye banh mi, falafel, injera—goodbye hot yoga, femme book clubs, "safe spaces." And she settled into her farmhouse a mile off the road from the nearest dying town. But she didn't want to live alone so she bought a special little circus breed dog and a couple of pigs. And she busied herself renovating the old barn into an apartment and scouted potential renters when she went into town.

She frequented J.J.'s, the local grocery store, because she often craved the tastes of her childhood like Cheez-Its and Mounds. And it was there that she met and fell in love with the checkout girl, Shania. And she quickly offered the young mother her barn apartment.

Shania moved in with her son and boyfriend. The boyfriend worked at the chicken factory. It was his job to hang up the birds by their feet and press the button for the machine to cut their heads off. The boy was three and he liked to play in the yard early in the mornings with the woman's little circus dog. The dog would jump and turn in the air for him and the boy would giggle.

Then the woman would wave goodbye to all of them when they left for town and wait for them at the window in the evenings until they got home.

But then one day a man came to install wifi at the woman's farm and she seduced him. She bathed him and braided his hair and traced his dragon tattoos with her tongue. And then he started sleeping there every night.

And sometimes they'd all get together in the woman's yard for shared cookouts. Shania would bring hamburger from work and her boyfriend would bring chickens and the wifi lover would cook them up on the grill. Shania and the woman would share a bottle of Barefoot pinot gris and the boy would chase lighting bugs with the little circus dog. Then the woman would always look up at the stars and say to the little boy, "You can see so many out here can't you?" "Yes," he would always squeal.

Spring turned to summer and summer turned to fall and, to keep herself from getting bored back in the country, the woman started chaining her lover up under the kitchen table for fun. It's one of those nights when she has the man chained down there naked, whipping his ass with a belt and making him bark, when they hear sirens coming from a long ways off, getting closer and closer.

The woman jumps to the window and watches a police car and then an ambulance fly up the path to her barn. The lights flash into the kitchen window, turning everything blue.

The woman unchains the man. And they throw on their heavy jackets, walk into their boots, and head out to see what's the matter. They are greeted by a policeman, one of her distant cousins, one she'd grown up with in school.

You can see his breath as he talks and this is what he tells them:

Shania called 911 about her son, she said he was choking on Kool-Aid. When the EMTs got there, the boy was in the middle of the living room floor, already purple. They went to perform mouth to mouth and when they cut open his little shirt to get to him better, they saw wounds all over his little body. It looked like the boy'd been choked with extension cords, whipped with a belt. Burns, deep, deep burns with pus all infected. And won't no bandages, look like they ain't never been cleaned. That little boy was neglected. Them wounds was trying to heal themselves. Ain't no telling what all he went through.

The policeman cousin clears his throat:

Shania done it, her boyfriend told us standing right there. And I ain't ever gonna forget how she looked at him while he was telling it. Just sick. Just pure evil…her own child.

The woman feels herself falling. She clings to the man's hip bone in the brown dry grass.

But the policeman cousin keeps going:

And then another little boy ran out from the back bedroom. Did y'all know she had twins?

The woman coughs, she chokes.

Yeah, she's got twins and was keeping one inside the house to beat on and taking the other one out into the world like there won't nothing wrong with it. Ain't no telling what that boy went through. He may not have even learned how to walk or talk or nothing. And none of her folks say they knew a thing about him.

The woman looks back towards the cop car and watches Shania bang her head against the window. Shania's son is squirming in the arms of another policeman, trying to get loose. He's watching his mama and crying. And the little circus dog is right there underneath him too, barking at the sound.

In the morning, the man leaves to install wifi. The woman feeds her pigs. And she walks through the tall grass to Shania's. She goes inside and lays down in the middle of the living room floor. She wants to know why the hell she never heard the boy crying when he was getting beaten and strangled, burned and bruised. Was he able to transcend? Turn into a spirit and leave his little body like an angel? Did he hover above himself, never looking down to see what was happening? Only up and smiling.

And Shania. Where is she now? In the county holding cell combing her fingers through her hair. And how does she feel knowing the little thing she could always beat on is gone?

A few days pass and the lover leaves and Shania's boyfriend goes to live with his family. The circus dog waits in the path to do tricks for the little boy, but the boy's riding a bus, being sent to a children's home in Raleigh.

The woman is alone again. She sits down and writes letters to all the unborn children her friends from college are carrying. In Kentucky, Minnesota, Ohio, Illinois. She stops to go outside and pick cotton fluff, something from home to send them. "Let them rub it under their noses," she writes. "That's what I did as a baby." The evening light falls in on her.

She walks all the way to the end of her path, puts the letters in the mailbox. She runs back to the house and climbs the magnolia tree as high as it'll take her. She screams out to her land. And if you keep pulling up, you'll lose her in the tree, but you'll see the moon shining on the tin roof of the farmhouse. The farm all alone, way outside town. The wilderness that surrounds them. The slick of the pigs' backs, moving in the dark. And even this far away, you can still hear her. And you can feel the boy near you, floating in stars.

Snowball Jr.

When I was a deer I was a doe. My mother pushed me out, nuzzling a great oak tree. It was spring. There was a creek nearby. Birds were always singing: meadowlark, grasshopper sparrow, nightingales. I could hear everything better than I'd ever heard before. But I didn't know if any loved ones from my old life were there with me. I missed them.

And I missed things I shouldn't have. I missed the man with stubby fingers, the smell of his awful butter lube. The peach-tiled bathroom. The vibrating bed and banana pudding milkshakes. The married man who called me Mama. He patched my tires, bought me groceries. Choked me in his ill-lit apartment during *Jeopardy*. Mad Dog 20/20. Omegle. Spit dangling from my lips onto his. Biting his rat tattoo.

I missed the man who looked like Bob Dylan on *Blonde on Blonde*. He wore paint-splattered jeans. We met in LAX. I handed him my copy of *VICE*. I told him to read the story "Malibu" about a man stuffing his fist into a stranger woman's mouth. It was a night flight and I watched the top of his hair glowing rows ahead. He was reading. It was thrilling.

But when I was a deer, the wind blew and I could smell the insides of flowers far away. I could hear cars coming like oceans. I could hear bees building hives.

In the summertime, me and mother ate from the soybean fields. That's where we liked eating best. It was open and easy, delicious and nice. And in the fall when I got bigger, my mother took me into the backyards of the country people. But only early in the morning when the sky was purple-pink and dew glistened on the apple trees. My deer mother would stretch her long neck and pick apples for me. I wanted to ask her—what did she hear? But I could only communicate with her in acts of service. This had also been my language before, rubbing Kiehl's Creme de Corps into his cracked knuckles, sweeping his floor; him filming me on my knees, my first video.

I let my deer mother clean me with her soft tongue. I drank her milk so gladly.

My mother before never nursed me. She never left the bed. She grew fatter and fatter every year of my youth. She stomped when she walked. I hated it. Once, we went to Disney and the Space Mountain attendant couldn't strap her in. She got a sleep apnea machine so the fat on her neck wouldn't smother her at night. She fed me Little Debbie cakes and chip sandwiches. Then she got gastric bypass, slimmed down, started wearing low cut tops and eyeshadow. She jumped from job to job, waitressing. She gossiped like middle school. The cooks and local policemen came by to see her on her shifts. Her necklaces got tangled in the skin tags on her neck. She begged me to mash cysts on her back. She could be so mean. She loved Prince and Lynyrd Skynyrd, *The Bachelorette* and Princess Di. She brought me a clean set of cotton panties when I got herpes. She didn't read, she didn't cook, she never cut her fingernails. Her daddy called her Snowball.

And I was Snowball Jr. I was a white-tailed deer, a doe. The apples I ate every fall were crisp and sweet. They smelled clean when I crunched them. It made my piss smell strong.

That's when the bucks started coming, they were rutting for me.

The first time I was mounted by a buck, I'd wandered far from home. I'd crossed two country roads to get to a patch of peanuts. And I laughed in my head, remembering when I was a little girl, my fat mama sat me down with a book called *Where Did I Come From?*

"Penis," it said. "Like Peanuts without the T!"

The buck smelled like oily hair and piss, akin to mine just mustier. And I wondered who the buck was, if he'd been anyone before. He could have been Napoleon, Cleopatra, or Mary Magdalene. Ted Bundy or Robert E. Lee.

When the married man filmed me on my knees he said I could make a lot of money. I needed a new set of tires and my wisdom teeth removed. He took out his pocket knife and cut through my tights. But this buck had trouble balancing. Every thrust pushed my front hooves further into the dirt. The land was dry and dusty. It was dark, but in my mind it was like a movie. I saw a spotlight shining from behind him, the shadow of his antlers, a piercing tangle before me. I heard the nightingales singing.

After the buck finished I started running back to my mother.

I couldn't really see, I was running so fast.

When I was little I played sick so I could stay home and cocoon myself in blankets. I'd poke my head out and watch the History Channel. As a form of meditation, Queen Elizabeth would translate English into Latin and then Latin back to English. She wrote a whole book of prayers that way. I was thinking of this, the steady stroke of her quill, when a car struck me.

I made it across the road but my insides started bleeding out of me. I fell in the lawn of a country church and a big rain came down. It fell into my eyes, onto my spongy tongue. The ground was getting soggy and I felt myself sink. I knew what would happen to me.

I'd seen it almost every day, the big black buzzards. When they got full they put out their wings and stood still as a statue, shining warm in the sun. But something I didn't know was the sound their feathers made when they were still. The wind pushing through their tight feathers made a long, high-pitched whistle.

But when I was a doe, I wanted my ending to be different. All I could think of was the great erotic Debussy composition. "Prélude à l'après-midi d'un faune." And I wished I could have been listening to it there while I died. From what I remember, in the beginning, there were harps and a french horn.

The Hunting Lodge

While Joyner Lee was away at college her car broke down. It needed a transmission rebuild. Her family couldn't help her. So she sold the good car parts she had for $500. Then she used the $500 to help her pay for books and get a good haircut. Joyner Lee studied English and she worked at the record store.

Her boss gave her a bike to ride back and forth to work with. So Joyner Lee rode for miles on the sides of the roads and on the little dirt foot paths when there were no sidewalks. She never hit a rock or got scraped up. Her legs got very strong. She was a very good record store salesperson.

Then one day, on the way home from the record store, a car full of men pulled up beside Joyner Lee at the stop light. They hung out the car windows and asked what kind of underwear she was wearing. She ignored them and waited for them to drive on so they wouldn't follow her home. She was on her period. She wanted to pull the bloody tampon out of her and sling it right into their sweaty laps.

After graduation, Joyner Lee moved back home and no one would hire her. Not even at the Family Dollar, Dollar General, or Dollar Tree. And it was really hard for her to talk to her family about all the things she missed back in the city, all the things she had seen. She had one aunt who read Amish Christian Romance novels. And everyone she knew went to church.

She became incredibly lonely and posted on her Instagram story almost anything she ever did throughout the day, like eating apples and putting her hair in ponytails. Then one day a writer commented on her Jack Kerouac post, a picture of his "40th chorus" from *San Francisco Blues*:

And when my head gets dizzy
And my friends all laugh
And money pours
    from my pocket
And gold from my ears
And silver flies out
    and rubies explode
I'll up & eat
And sing another song
And drop another grape
    In my belly down

"That's a God one," he commented.
"Good one," she commented back.

She laughed and he sent her a dm.

"My name is Sam," he said.

"Well guess what, Sam," Joyner Lee said, "I don't live that far from Rocky Mount. Rocky Mount's my nearest bookstore. That's where Jack Kerouac lived."

"Yes, I know," Sam said. "But tell me about you—I want to hear the whole story."

So she started at the beginning and when she got to the end he sent her a picture of his shoulder. He was in the bath. She could see half his face and his lips were beautiful. His name was Sam and Joyner Lee fell in love with him.

Summer turned to fall and her cousin said he'd pay her some money if she'd clean his hunting lodge in between hunters, so mostly a two-day-a-week gig, but it was better than nothing. So Joyner Lee stripped the beds and washed the sheets and towels. She scrubbed the kitchen floors. She stood up on the top of a stool and swiffered inside the bobcat's mouth, cleaning cobwebs from his teeth. And she picked bottles of deer piss off the bathroom floor.

She sent Sam pictures of everything. Told him how hunters used deer piss to attract deer. And the differences between button heads, toe heads, and bucks. "Wow," he said. He sent her heart eyed smiley faced emojis. And gasp emojis that made her laugh. He lived in L.A. and ran on the tops of mountains. He sent pictures to her of dry valleys and shrub-lined paths. She thought it looked biblical like Damascus Road. "Holy, holy, holy," Sam said.

They found out they both were horses in the Chinese Zodiac. Which meant they were both charming, intellectual, and free. So Joyner Lee started running too, into the woods behind the lodge, when she was done cleaning. She'd jump over mudholes and snakes. And she'd always search for turkeys because that was Sam's favorite word: turkey. He loved the way it felt in his mouth when he said it. She loved the way he said it. He spoke so precisely and correct. He'd call her from bar bathrooms, sometimes even his bedroom late at night. He lived with his parents but was moving to Nashville soon. She'd never been anywhere he was. She'd never been anywhere he was going to.

She put the money she earned in a purple Crown Royal bag under her mattress. She lived alone in an old house. And houses in her neighborhood were getting broken into all the time. Her cousin helped her keep her propane tank filled for heat so she wouldn't freeze and he told her she needed a gun.

Fall turned to winter and sometimes after cleaning, if her sister couldn't pick her up, Joyner Lee'd get rides into town with the old men in their rattly cars. The men told her they remembered her when she was little, playing in yards. They'd tell her the nicknames of old dead family members she never knew. Everything would smell like thick exhaust with the gospel radio blaring. And she'd remember some of the songs, the words coming back to her through hurts past and present. She was happy she had Sam now. Joyner Lee asked them but none of the old men had ever been to Nashville either. One of them gave her a pair of fuzzy gloves. And her cousin gave her deer sausage and sweet potatoes to eat, so she wouldn't have to buy groceries.

Sam sent her books about mermaids and Paris and a postcard with blue maned horses that said, "Horsing Around in Nashville Town." He said his family would love her. He said they'd all get along. He said he'd take her to his neighbor's New Years Eve party. Every morning she looked forward to a text from him saying BABY BABY. And a call from him saying she was the real deal every night.

Sam believed Joyner Lee was a writer. But Joyner Lee never wrote. She was squirting windex into mounted buck eyes and drying dishes. She was taking out the trash. She was saving up for a plane ticket to Nashville, dreaming of turkeys, wiping her nose on her fuzzy gloves. Every day he worked on a novel and she immediately read any of it he sent to her. He was always using words in ways she'd never seen, words she'd never known. Sentences that looped upon each other again and again like a big spiritual circle she didn't understand. Sam asked her if she believed in quantum entanglement. He believed they were connected.

It was cold in Joyner Lee's house. In the mornings, she saw her breath. As mentioned before, she lived alone, and didn't have anyone there to talk to. She wrote a note on her fridge that said:

Keep going for
- the boy who loves turkeys
- Nashville
- a new car
- and future kids someday

The only place Joyner Lee had cell phone reception at the lodge was under the cleaning shed. So while the winter birds cooed in the dry cornstalks and the tall grasses swished, she stood under the cleaning shed holding her cell phone, waiting to reach Sam. Wherever he was, somewhere warm, somewhere in Nashville, propped against a jukebox with a beer in his hand.

But here under the cleaning shed, when Joyner Lee looked up she saw the hanging racks. And every time she always remembered one of the most beautiful things she'd ever seen and how it happened there. When she was a little girl, her cousin killed a bear and her family went out to the lodge to see it. It was late at night and her and her sister stood there in their pajamas and heavy jackets. Another cousin held a floodlight so everyone could see. And they hung the bear up by his front paws on the rack while another cousin cranked him up into the air. The big black bear hung there suspended in the cold night. Her cousin took the knife then and cut him from his private parts to his throat. His skin was pulled so tight across his ribs that it came apart like velcro. It sounded like velcro too. And his insides plopped out of him so fast onto the concrete below. A wet plop, a pile of purple red mush steaming and shining. The heat looked like smoke. Her mama shook like she had the heebee jeebees. "C'mon, let's go," she said. But Joyner Lee wanted to stay there all night to see it. She knew she'd never see it again and she wanted to see everything. She didn't want to forget.

Joyner Lee knew there was no way she could ever tell Sam this in a way he could understand. She stripped the beds and washed the towels, scrubbed the bathroom floors. She didn't see any turkeys. Sam said that was fine. Sam said he was coming to visit, that he'd cook her a very good curry and they'd take a trip to see old Jacky's house in Rocky Mount. One day they'd go to Paris too and name their child Roy.

Then Sam stopped sending Joyner Lee books and heart eyes and gasping faces. And then he stopped wanting to hear what she thought about things. And he never came to visit. At night she pulled the covers over her head. She dreamed of Sam sitting in the middle of her bedroom on a stool.

Joyner Lee ran behind the lodge farther than she ever had before. She ran until she came to the dump pile of animal pieces. A little mountain of white, white bones. Deer legs and button head skulls, teeth and sometimes patches of hair, tall grass growing through eyes. She dug through them and found her favorite pieces. And she took pictures of herself holding skulls, smiling as big as she could. The vultures watched her from the trees. Everyone was hungry. And in the end, when it was all said and done, no one liked Sam's novel anyway.

The Virgin

When I wake up my iPhone won't turn on and the nearest Apple place is in Norfolk at the mall and that's an hour and a half away. I put on a bright lipstick, brush my hair, and rub my wrists with one of them perfume samples from the paper. It's spicy and sweet.

On the ride there, my car pulls to the right. My right tire's been leaking air for a while now. The radio plays "When Doves Cry" by Prince.

Before Weston left me, he put me in handcuffs and held my head underwater in the bathtub. I would have done anything for him. I pass fields and then the fields turn to nice houses and traffic.

In the parking deck the car beside me has brand-new tires. I run my fingers over the treads. I've never had much money. This iPhone Weston gave me is the only nice thing I really got. I can't afford to heat my house. I don't have any friends. Bri and the rest of them stopped talking to me when Weston moved us across the river.

The people in the mall move in clusters. They huddle outside the Cheesecake Factory. They're wearing clothes like what's on the mannequins. Their shoes look new too.

The only house we could afford across the river was an old mill house. It'd been sitting there abandoned for three years before we moved in. Neighborhood kids came in and kicked the railing out the staircase. They wrote fuck on the dining room wall. Birds built nests in the ceiling fans. Every night I sleep under six blankets and wear two sweaters, pants, and socks. I have one

electric heater and I blast it towards my head. And I hope these folks in the mall can't see that when they look at me.

The man at the Apple store who helps me is named Chris. The store is real busy. Lots of folks are talking and walking around. Sometimes when Weston's friends would come to visit, he'd film me having sex with them. "Come for me, baby," he'd say. I didn't want to be with anyone but him.

Me and Chris look down at my iPhone on the table in front of us.

"I just need this fixed please," I say.

Chris says he understands. I'd like for him to hug me.

I tell him I don't have much money. I tell him I sweep hair at a salon.

"It's okay," Chris says and then he looks me in the eye and says, "We're gonna get you straight."

Chris takes my iPhone with him and goes away for a while.

I pull my pants up from where they're getting big on me and touch my lips to see if my lipstick's still there and it is, but I can feel it getting dry and flaky.

It doesn't take long for Chris to come back with a new iPhone. "Looks like it was a manufacturing malfunction. Unfortunately, your phone was a bad egg," he says. "But fortunately, it's still under warranty. You're getting a brand-new phone for free." He takes the new iPhone out of the box.

I tell him how thankful I am. I tell him how much I appreciate it.

"I'll just need your password to get you set up," Chris says.

"Weston," I say real quick, like it don't mean nothing.

Chris looks at me and then back at the phone. "So let's see, that makes it…"

"Nine three seven, eight six six."

While everything's syncing up Chris asks me if I like sweeping hair. He says it sounds relaxing. Then he asks me where I'm from.

"The way you say some of your words, it's different. I think it's pretty cool," he says.

"Well, this is how everybody talks back home," I say. I feel flattered.

But when I tell him where I'm from, of course, he's never heard of it. Nobody ever has.

"Well, before you head back," he says, "you should check out the art museum. It's free and I go there on my days off."

Chris's hands look kind; they look gentle. They're big and he has dark hair on his knuckles.

"It's a really special spot," he says. "I think you'll like it."

I've never been to an art museum before, but I tell him I'll check it out. He smiles at me and tells me it was nice to meet me. He wishes me a safe drive home and tells me to enjoy the museum.

I tell him goodbye and go wander around the beauty section in Dillard's. I find the perfume like what I'm wearing on display and I spray some more on. I find a new color of Estée Lauder lipstick that I like and put that on too. It's called "Bold Innocent." A woman behind the counter with shiny skin tells me how pretty my complexion is. She wants to give me a free beauty consultation, but I tell her I'm shy and walk away. I don't like strangers to touch me.

On the way to the car I pass the food court and see Chris ordering a smoothie. He puts his hair back in a ponytail while he waits for it. When they call his name, he smiles and waves his hand up. "That's me," he says. It's a blue smoothie. Blueberries, I guess.

The walkway to the museum winds through a front yard filled with mirrors. One reflects a small pond. I stand in front of it and wave at myself. I pull out my new iPhone and take a picture of myself waving in the mirror.

The first things I see inside the museum are special ancient toothbrushes and little glass pieces of jewelry shaped like lion heads and butterflies. Then I look at statues of Chinese warriors and people from Italy. I see lots of paintings. There's benches in front of some of them for you to sit and look. Some people are sitting there writing in notebooks. I sit in front of a big painting of a naked girl, laying on the ground with a flower in her hand and a little dog on her chest. The mountains behind her are purple and the sky is pink. Her hair is brown. And there's people in the distance, way back on this path coming around the mountain, heading towards her.

I miss Bobby Labonte. He was my dog when I was little, named after my favorite racecar driver. He used to lick my legs when I got out the shower. I'd roll around with him in the yard and we'd both come up with ticks. He'd let me pull cockleberries out of his thick fur.

And I've never been to the mountains, but I bet I would like them too. I've always wanted to go to Dollywood.

I get up and see who painted the naked girl with the dog on her chest. I can't pronounce his name. It's something foreign, but it starts with a G. The name of the painting is "The Virgin." I take a picture of it on my phone.

When I leave the art museum, it's raining, and my windshield wipers need replacing. It's scary driving through the traffic with all the lights reflecting on the road and blurring through the wipers. But I make it back to the country, where I know the roads. I pass the old houses I always see rotting back in fields and think about the hole in my living room floor that I stuffed with newspaper. When it rains hard like this you can look down the hole and see the water running beneath the house. I think I'll eat me a sweet potato for supper, maybe take my clothes up town to wash them. They normally got the TV in there on a Lifetime movie on Monday nights. Last week a girl was kidnapped by this crazy man who thought he was Jesus and he tied her to a tree in the woods.

Last night before I went to sleep, I thought I saw Weston standing out under the streetlight looking in at me in the window. I called one of my cousins who lives the town over to see if she could drive by and see. But she said it was past midnight dammit and she won't driving around where I live that late at night. She told me it was nothing. She told me to go to sleep.

My right tire pops outside the nursing home about forty-five minutes from my house. And I call my cousin who's got a wrecker. He says he can't get there for another hour and a half but to hold tight. I'm outside in the rain looking at my tire torn to shreds trying to figure who I can ask for money for a new one when I hear a woman hollering at me to come inside. I look towards the nursing home and she's there holding the door open for me.

When I get to her, she asks me if I'm all right, if I need a ride somewhere.

I tell her I'm fine, that my cousin will be here to get me.

Her nurse scrubs has dogs having a tea party on them. They're drinking out of tea cups and wearing hats and everything. She calls me sugar and tells me to stand right there. She's gonna bring me a towel and a change of clothes.

"This is pneumonia catching weather," she says. "Poor thing, you're soaked like a lil rat."

She runs down the hall and I'm dripping onto the floor. I'm shivering, but everything in here is clean. A man in a wheelchair smiles at me from the corner. The windows have nice long curtains and there's paintings of beaches on the walls.

Weston's cousin had a trailer down at Kitty Hawk. He took me there a couple of times. We went fishing on Jennette's pier and I caught a shark.

The nurse comes back, hands me a towel and dry clothes.

"And put your wet clothes in this," she says, offering me a trash bag.

She points me to the guest bathroom and I look back at the man in the corner. He's pushing his feet against the floor, trying to scooch his wheelchair in my direction. The nurse goes to him and squats down in front of his knees. He stops and looks at her, then he looks back at me. "We've sure got a pretty visitor don't we, Mr. Pipeman?" she says. He doesn't say anything, but the nurse turns to me, smiling. "You know, we're about to have supper down the hall," she says, "and I'm the supervisor of that wing and I want you to come eat with us. We've got enough to feed an army." She starts to push Mr. Pipeman down the hall. "How's that sound to you, huh?" she says to him. She motions her head towards the wing's double doors. "And see this doorbell here? Ring it when you're ready and we'll let you in. We'll have a place set for ya."

The clothes have the name A. REYNOLDS written inside the collar of the sweater and in the waist of the pants. The sweater is printed in yellow and pink flowers and the pants are pink corduroy with elastic at the waist. They come up to my belly button like old lady pants do, but they're really soft. The socks are purple and fuzzy and have the things on the bottom that keep you from slipping.

At supper I sit down between two little ladies, one with long hair pulled back in a bumblebee barrette and one with cheery big eyes like a Disney character. They both are going through pocketbooks in their laps like they're looking for something. Then a nurse wheels Mr. Pipeman, from before, to sit across from me and he seems to be the only one at the table that notices me until Mrs. Bumblebee drops her pocketbook on the floor and asks me what my name is.

I tell her and then she tells me her name is Reeby.

And then the Disney woman tells me her name is Mrs. Creech and slaps Mr. Pipeman lightly on the arm and says, "This here is Mr.Pipeman. Tell her hello, Pipeman."

He doesn't look at me. He stares at the flowers on my sweater.

Then Mrs. Creech giggles and tells me she loves the color of my lipstick. "What's it called?" she asks.

"Bold Innocent," I say, and she acts like I wrote the name on her heart.

"I always wore Crimson in Snow," Reeby says. "My husband loved it. He was in the Navy. He spoke French."

"Are you married?" Mrs. Creech asks me all giddy-like.

"Yes," I tell them. "His name is Chris. He works in the mall. He speaks French, too. He even took me to Paris for our honeymoon."

"Ain't that something," Reeby says.

The dog tea party nurse brings our supper by and gives me a big grin and tells me she's happy I could join them. Supper is mashed potatoes, hamburger steak, snaps, gravy, and fruit cocktail. The food is so good and I'm at the best table in the dining room. There are folks at other tables sleeping and slobbering and nurses are yelling at them to open their mouths.

Weston wanted me to fuck him in the ass. He bought me a dildo to use on him. But he wanted me to put my fingers in him first. We tried to in the shower, but he kept saying my fingernails hurt him. He liked me to keep my nails long and painted because he said they looked good around his cock.

I look at my fingernails now, plain and unpainted, bitten down to the quick. Chris likes to order blueberry smoothies. He likes to wear black pants. He likes museums. He speaks French.

Mrs. Creech leans in then and asks me how old I am.

I tell her and Reeby says I don't look a day older than seventeen. She says, "You ain't nothing but a spring chicken." She pokes at the cherry in her fruit cocktail and says she's ninety-seven.

Mrs. Creech has got her elbows on the table now, resting her head in her hands towards me. She asks me what my name is again.

I tell her my name is Lacy.

Then she tells me her name again and slaps Mr. Pipeman on the arm again and says, "This here is Mr. Pipeman."

"Nice to meet y'all," I say.

Reeby eats a grape from her fruit cocktail.

"My husband was in the Navy," she says. "He spoke French. His family was from Canada."

Mrs. Creech tells me she loves my hair. She says she's always tried to get hers to do that.

And she asks me how old I am again.

"Well, gosh," Reeby looks up at me. "You don't look a day older than seventeen." Then she looks back down at the fruit cocktail and says she's ninety-seven.

I don't know where Weston is now. I haven't heard from him since January. He called me from a hotel in Charlotte, told me I was a dirty whore, a piece of shit, and said he never wanted to hear from me again. He told me that when he went out to fancy bars he put a pair of my panties in his coat like a pocket square.

Reeby looks at Mrs. Creech and asks her how old she is.

Mrs. Creech says she can't remember.

"Well, when's your birthday?" Reeby reaches for her hand on the table.

And Mrs. Creech takes her hand and hangs her head and shakes it.

Weston was the first man I ever let touch me. I loved him. He told me he loved me.

Another nurse comes by and brings all my new friends their medicine in little cups.

Mrs. Creech and Reeby let go of each other's hands and take their cups.

"Oh look, honey," Reeby says to Mrs. Creech, "our birth control!" She looks at me grinning and winks before she throws the pills back like a shot.

"Yes," Mrs. Creech laughs like she forgot she was ever sad before. "Yes, this is my birth control, too!" She throws hers back and then asks me where mine is.

I tell her I don't need it.

"I'm a virgin," I say. "My name's Lacy and I'm a virgin. I speak French."

They smile at me like it's the only truth there ever was. It's nice and I'm warm and full. Everyone tells me they love me before I go.

The Truth About
Miss Katie

I didn't like it when I heard what Miss Katie said at her going away party. And I probably shouldn't have been listening but I wanted to tell her goodbye. At the party she said, "Excuse me I have a phone call," and then she didn't come back in for a long time so I went out the bleachers where she always talks on the phone because she says that's where she has best reception and I wish I didn't hear her. What she said. She didn't know I was there. And that was rude I guess and not good manners but Miss Katie is my favorite person—or was—because she's smart and pretty and always has her nails done nice and she told me that one time that my bush baby I did was looking so cute in the bush.

I had never done art before, I mean I'd seen it on TV like on Disney Channel and the Miley Cyrus show when she had to do a thing called a self-portrait. But that's why I loved when Miss Katie came. I just wanted to try art. You hear about it in all the stories, people painting, looking at paintings. I know that paintings are in museums because the library book I checked out told me about it. I've never been to a museum before either.

I heard that in the 6th grade we can go see a museum on the big field trip that the 6th graders take. They take us up to UNC to see the basketball court where Michael Jordan played and then they take us to a museum. We got to raise money to get up there though because we have to get this real big bus to take us and you have to get there real early at six in the morning and you CAN NOT be late. Or you'll be holding up your friends!

So I wanted to do this art. And I had never heard of a bush baby before either until Miss Katie came and read us that story about Africa and she showed us how to draw animals from Africa in white crayon on white paper. And I know that sounds crazy because how are you gonna see anything with white crayon on white paper? But when you put the watercolor on it, it shows up really good. Well like I said, Miss Katie said I did so good on my bush baby, "Pretty eyes," she said. "Between you and me it's the best one in the class." And that made me feel good.

When I got my period I thought I was hurt and I didn't know what was happening to me and I was crying in the bathroom stall at school and Miss Katie came in there and told me I was okay. She said I should be proud, that it meant I was becoming a young lady. She said she had one too. And she gave me a pad to put in my panties. And when Grandma picked me up from school that day Miss Katie walked out with me to Grandma's car and held my hand and she said, "Your granddaughter got her period today at school and I hope I didn't overstep my boundaries or anything but she didn't know what was going on and she was scared…" And then Grandma interrupted her and said, "That girl needs to feel scared." I could tell Miss Katie didn't know what to say then.

My Grandma is the bossy type. More bossy than Miss Katie. She don't let us keep the lights on at night because of the electric bill and so when the sun goes down me and brother and sister sit in our room in the dark just talking to each other and sometimes my baby sister is afraid and I hold her and scratch her back real light like you're barely touching her to get her to go to sleep. You can't do it too hard or it won't work. And Grandma won't send me to school but with one pad. She says they're expensive. So I told Miss Katie and she brought some pads to school just for me. And now whenever I feel the blood coming out of me I can change pads as much as I want. I hate feeling like I'm sitting in my own blood.

But Miss Katie said that I was a smart girl, a curious person, and that meant I was exciting. Miss Katie says to be normal is one of the most boring things in life. She taught us paper ma-shay. She has a paper ma-shay of her boobs that she keeps in her desk, she showed it to me one time.

She said I was a real artist. She really liked everything I'd paint. "Good color choice," that's something she always said. She said that on my self-portrait. That's also when she told me I was beautiful. "See," and she pointed to my face and said, "This is just beautiful."

Miss Katie made me want to be a teacher. She taught me so much. And I wanted to tell her goodbye. I wanted to tell her how nice I think she is and thank her for all she's done and ask her if she thinks we'll ever see each other again.

I wanted to give her a gift. I wanted to paint her a painting. A thing called a still life, of opening spring flowers, but she never even got around to staying around here long enough for me to see any spring flowers open. And I didn't want to ask Grandma for a canvas. Grandma wouldn't even let me explain what a canvas was. She said, "None of that mess."

So I stole some paper from school and did a self-portrait at night in my room in the dark. I had to try it over and over again for a while like that until it came out good. Because I couldn't really see what all I was doing, but I got the hang of it after a while. And that's what I wanted to give her, the self-portrait I did, because it had gummy worms on it, floating around my head.

Miss Katie asked me what was my favorite restaurant and I said that even though I love McDonald's, and McDonald's has toys 'cause my cousin Terri works there and she brings them to us from her work, I have never been to the Golden Corral. I've seen the commercials and I don't even know where it is around here but the TV says that the Golden Corral is all you can eat—it's buffet. Kayla says she's been there and that buffet means the food never goes out. You can eat until you're so full you're about to pop. Kayla says if I ever go, to try the BBQ pizza. She says you wouldn't think it, cause it sounds gross, but she says it's so so good.

Miss Katie said she'd never gone to the Golden Corral, but she said that she'd take me someday. I told her I heard we can put candy on our ice cream there. "I'm sure," she said. She said she'd put gummy worms on her ice cream. And I just wanted to know if she could tell me when I went out to the bleachers to find her and give her my self-portrait when we were going to go to the Golden Corral.

But when I got out there, I saw her on the phone and I didn't want to interrupt. I listened behind the gym, heard her talking some real bad stuff. She was saying, "This place is a shit hole." And, "I'm just so alone here." And she told her friend that we'd made her a 7Up cake. Miss Katie was kinda laughing then. She said she spit the cake out in the bathroom. She said 7Up cake was some country shit.

I can't believe she said that. I mean she told us that she loved the 7Up cake. And it really is so good. We never get it except only on special occasions when Sammy's mama makes it. We all love it so much when she makes it. It's my favorite cake.

Miss Katie said the swimming pool here doesn't even have a diving board. I'd never thought about that before, but she said it so mean. And she said she was scared of getting robbed. She was shaking her head and getting frustrated. "Yeah, you're right," she said. "Helping. Yes. They needed me." Yeah she did show us things, but I never knew that we needed any help.

Miss Katie started crying on the phone and I remembered my sister. She'd be crawling into the fridge at night when she was hungry, when she won't supposed to be looking for something to eat. It hurt my feelings to hear Miss Katie talk like that. And I want to tell her that I don't ever want her to come back here again because I hate her.

The Chopping Block

This feels like a really long shower, the way the water's moving down my body. Maybe it's because my eyes are closed. I move my tongue in my mouth and think that hole in my gums is getting bigger. I don't know how it happened or what it's for. I'm too high to be able to tell if I'm just high as hell or really falling into another depressive episode. Like getting pulled by an undercurrent and not knowing when I can come up for air. Riding around this morning, I thought I ought to press that pocket knife into my skin some to see how fast the blood would come out. I did take note of that.

And I am fully aware I ain't even washing, just standing in the water, rinsing off. My sister's damn pool has so many pine needles and leaves, moss floating at the bottom. That's where I swam to, tried to see if I could lay down there in it. Rub my belly on it. I figured it would be soft.

"Don't you get into that water. It's September," my sister hollered off the back porch. "You'll get pneumonia."

I almost died from double pneumonia when I was in first grade.

But I told her if she don't want a pool in September then to get her lazy ass up and take it down. Her damn boyfriend won't do it, that old fucker. He's old enough to be our damn daddy. When I came in the house that fucker was sitting there looking at *Wheel of Fortune*.

I looked right in his face when I came in and told him that nasty water felt good.

"I reckon it did," he said.

Back at my old place it was hard. It was like when you come out of the shower and you're so cold and you want to be warm and you dig through your drawer for some pants and you pull out his pants, your man's pants, 'cause you've felt him in them before.

'Cause you've been riding around looking over to your right wanting to feel his knuckles between your teeth. But you haven't seen your man in months and you don't know when you'll ever see him again.

◊ ◊ ◊

"Let me see your eyes," the old fucker says to me from the recliner.

I bend down low enough in front of him that he could yank the towel right off of me there if he wanted to. Strange for a sister to be living with her sister and her sister's boyfriend but that's what I've been doing. And I knew this fucker was a dick before, but now it's just more apparent.

He's a piece of shit. Sister's tires are slick as anything and she's got to drive to Hertford County to work back and forth everyday and he won't give her no money to help her get new tires. That's something My Man would never do. He always paid for my mama's meal every time we went up to the café for Sunday lunch. Made me so mad when I found out that old fucker was letting my mama pay for his Sunday lunch.

The old fucker cuts his hair close to his head to hide that he's balding. With my sister so young and pretty he wants to fit in. But I can see the bald spots looking pale from the TV.

"You're crazy as hell," he says.

"That's right," I tell him.

He calls my sister from the kitchen.

She comes in cradling a bowl of potatoes she's steady mashing.

"I told you, just look at her. High as a damn kite," he says it like I ain't there.

My hair is dripping wet on my shoulders. Collecting in my collarbones. I'm getting cold.

Old fucker says if I won't kin he'd take me to Jackson and throw me in jail. He's a state trooper. He thinks he's hot shit. He says if he goes in the bathroom again and there's weed ashes on the counter. He says weed like "weeeeeeeeeeeeed."

My sister stops him and looks at me like she's saying "Why" but instead she says, "Go on and put some clothes on. Supper will be ready here presny." "Presny" is an old word we learned from the old people in our family who raised us.

My sister loves me. But we're really different. We disagree on things she don't understand. Like if I got pregnant, she don't understand how I couldn't at least carry the baby. See, I couldn't carry it and have it and give it up for adoption. I'd want to hold it and then I'd want to keep it. So that's why I'd need an abortion. But Sister thinks that's wrong.

My sister keeps the bulletins from all the children's funerals she's gone too. She keeps them in the side pocket of her car. I never knew that until one time on the way to church I was talking about something I don't remember now. About life not being fair probably, but that it's only our one life to live, and she pulled them bulletins out at the stop sign and showed them to me. She works at a daycare. She knows lots of children. She said, "This family has lost an innocent child. They had their whole life ahead of them."

She also clearly believes in God and she believes in the best in people. When she prays to God she feels better. But not me. Maybe that is part of my problem—I have not gone to the Lord about My Man yet.

My sister has a full length mirror behind her bedroom door. I like to look at my full self naked there. I've got a dark hair growing out of my left nipple and I pull it out. Then I think I want someone to choke me. Or bite my lip until it bleeds. I'd like someone to slap me in the face. It's good seeing how much you can take. It'll surprise you. The more it hurts, the better it feels when you're finally released.

But no man can touch me now. Only My Man.

I'm all hairy everywhere now. No need to shave because I am a nun except when I masturbate and that is like cosmic sex above me. That is when I remember the time like, for example, when we walked into my kitchen and My Man picked me up and then on the counter, then kitchen table, then floor. It was dark and the porch light came in from the window. He picked me up in his arms then and was in me from under so fast. I was in the air, flying like magic.

Last time I masturbated I touched myself to the idea that all my dead family I knew and loved were reunited in heaven. And they weren't watching me but they were on a big TV being happy together and hugging each other. And I was watching them and I was very happy. It was nice to see them smiling with each other. They missed each other so much when they were alive.

I put on a real skimpy tank top and Soffe shorts Sister used to wear for softball practice, something to show my scars from where I was in the hospital in that freak accident where they fucked me up when they were taking out my appendix, that's a whole 'nother story but I'll tell ya this: I laid there for three months and My Man came to kiss me on the forehead and tell the nurses I needed more morphine. They shot it straight into my veins, right into my arms. The fat redheaded nurse shot it in me the fastest and that always felt best, like a band of angels was beating their wings so graceful together at the top of my head, making warm waves come down into my body. I'd wake up to people from church at the end of my bed, praying. Or Daddy shaking his head, saying I was cut open like a hog.

When I was twelve, my cousin gave me a *Norton Anthology of American Literature* she used in college. That was the first time I saw a poem that didn't rhyme. That was the first time I read Sylvia Plath. An associates in arts from Halifax Community College don't get you much nowhere, but I wrote all my papers on *Ariel* anyways. That's when I read "Lady Lazarus" and "Fever 103." *All by myself I am a huge camellia, glowing and coming and going, flush on flush.* I didn't know what that meant then but I thought it sounded magnificent. And I felt sad for no reason.

"Take it easy, just don't worry so much," Mama said when I was so afraid of the Book of Revelations at night when I was a little girl and would cry and cry. She'd have to hold me until I fell asleep. I just kept thinking about the floor ripping open. Looking outside and seeing fire coming down. Raining fire outside the window.

And that's one of the things, I think. My Man claimed he was an atheist. He said he didn't need anyone or anything to pull him out of trouble. He said he just needed himself. How if his legs had just got broken and he was on the road in the middle of the desert, without a phone, if he remembered someone said to dig a hole with your ring finger and spit in it and mix it around five whole times that you'd survive and get out of that desert, he said he wouldn't do it. On a documentary about the Holocaust I saw one time, the filmmaker asked the old lady survivor if she believed in God and she said, "When you're drowning you'll reach for the tiniest straw." My Man said he won't gonna reach for nothing.

And then I didn't tell him I'd been feeling my heart pulling towards another and I laid down with that other one night and I didn't let him touch me but that other told me how we're all made of stars and we really do make up the universe and are made of the universe and how powerful and lonely that felt at the same time and how that's the origin of the species and only then did I remember My Man. I had never heard that before and I was afraid. I went back to My Man and didn't tell him about it.

I met My Man online. We matched on OKCupid. He misspelled *The Picture of Dorian Gray* in his profile. I've never read it but had enough sense to know how it's spelled. So I told him. And then he had a good strong name and then he asked for my number and then he was gonna see me for New Year's Eve but he got in a wreck on the way to see me. I didn't know to believe him or not. But it was true. He totaled his truck but he made it out without a scratch.

Then we met in real life kinda on a Google Hangout. I could hear his voice and see how it came out of him. He was sitting on his living room sofa showing me all these little vases and samurai swords. His granddaddy had been an international antique dealer. Sacred soap stones from India. It's like he had them all in a pile sitting next to him on the couch where I couldn't see. I was waiting for a shrunken head, for him to hold it by the hair and spin it in front of the camera. He kept bringing them up, asking me if I could see them, as if to say, "Look at this, look at this."

All I know is the girl he's seeing now lives in Asheboro and that's where the zoo is. And I bet you a million dollars they've already been there. He drives up on a Friday night in that dirty ass stick shift truck I promised him I'd clean for his birthday. Filled with papers and receipts and bags and clothes and towels and camping gear. Listens to cassettes I used to surprise him with all the time, like Hank Williams. Driving up there and taking her out to a good dinner. I seen on Facebook that she's got pink hair. I hope he doesn't get so excited talking to her like he would with me, talking so fast he'd have to stop and suck in that little bit of slobber that was about to drip out his mouth. Them nice lips so pretty that I cry. I hope she don't sound as good as me when they kiss. When she climbs him like a monkey in the kitchen like I used to do. Putting his head under my chin and reaching for the cumin, he'd laugh and say it, "Coming."

He'd go with me to visit Daddy in the nursing home. Be there to put his hand on my back. Daddy is sick with a disease I don't wanna mention because I don't want you to try to relate to me or say your grandma had it. I don't want you to feel sorry for me. And because of this disease Daddy is still dying of, Daddy never knew My Man's name. But before Daddy forgot how to talk, he said he liked My Man. I sat next to Daddy and he said, "He'd do anything for you, if you asked him."

And then My Man wakes up in the morning with that Asheboro girl's head on his chest. And I get so sick thinking about it. And then they go to the zoo and look at the seals swimming in the water. They stop and ask an elderly but energetic couple to take their picture. One of those nice couple pictures you see all the time, where they stand together smiling, his hand on her waist and her hand placed on his stomach, as if she's holding him back. My Man is so handsome. They tell the nice old lady to take a couple of pictures because they want a seal behind them in it. My Man makes a joke. He's good with all sorts of people. I hope they don't get the seal in the picture.

Next thing I know I am half way under my sister's bed, just laying here with my eyes closed. Maybe I am meditating. It's nice down here, like being in a coffin.

I heard a story once about getting buried alive. They accidentally buried the man face down and he woke up and clawed and clawed at the coffin. Clawing to hell in a way. And his ghost came to his best friend's bedside for three nights in a row telling him to come and dig him up. When they finally did and they dug him up and saw how afraid his dead face looked in the eyes, they buried him right side up. And from then on caskets was made with a rounded top to them.

I thought about that story when we were at Aunt Ginny's wake the other day. And I thought, I'm glad they are burying her right side up so she'll be looking towards heaven. Or at the Second Coming when she sits up, she'll just be able to step right on out. She looked so pretty in the casket and I felt bad I never went to visit her more than I did when she got real bad down in the bed. Her hip bone had pushed through her skin. Her legs were stuck in fetal position. But she fit in the casket so I guess they broke them to get her in there right. I didn't ask.

◊ ◊ ◊

My sister has all of Daddy's little model airplanes he built. She's got them in special shelves in her living room. The old fucker says we could sell them for good money and Sister went behind my back and gave him some to sell. That burned me up so bad. That fucker kept the damn money and bought a new gun for the first day of dove season.

That couple on Chestnut Street got Daddy's chopping block he was so proud of. That he got when the butcher uptown closed. He loved that damn thing. Mama hated it 'cause it took up so much room in the kitchen. Right there in the middle of the kitchen. That's where they pinned me down to make me swallow medicine. And that's where we ate watermelon. Daddy would take our hands and show us, make us feel where the wood had worn down and got deep, where the meat had been cut up the most. We don't really know the folks who have it. I mean like who all they came from. They got it when the bank took the house after Daddy got sick and we went bankrupt. Don't know how much Mama sold it for. I bet for not enough.

I smell that Sister's started frying the pork chops. I push myself out from under the bed and look at myself in the mirror again before I head down the hall. My sister is making what I liked to eat when I was little. Mashed potatoes and then you put some peas in the middle and call it "eggs in a basket."

I'm opening a can of Le Sueur peas when she says to me, "You know I thought you and that nice looking guy you were always so close to in high school would make a good couple. You and him."

She flips a pork chop. "He always played that guitar so good. What did he play, that "Hotel California" song at all the home games?"

"Exactly." I pour the peas in the pot. "That's basic. The Eagles."

"He's moving back soon, you know? From grad school to work on his daddy's tree farm," she says. "As pretty as you are. I know he'd love to go out with you. Slim pickings round here."

This is the first time my Sister has ever talked to me like this, pushing some man on me.

I finally tell her I'm writing a letter to My Man. I haven't told no one. I've taken all summer to do it. I'm afraid to send it. I don't want it to be the last time I talk to him.

"What all does it say?" She reaches in the cabinet for plates.

"What's in my heart," I tell her. "How every time I dream about him I wake up crying." I can feel myself starting to fall to pieces.

"Maybe it's better if you let it ride, let it play itself out." Sister puts the plates on the table and puts her hand on my arm. "He's already seeing someone else, Sister. I mean it's been what, like, almost a year?"

And I fall to pieces right there in the kitchen floor. And my sister's there, picking me up, telling me it's time for me to be taking care of myself. "We don't need no man," she says. She's wiping my face with a warm dishrag. "We're strong, Sister," she says.

And that's when the old fucker walks in and asks me if I ran off my meds again and if I need money for the damn refill. If I was that tight for money he'd fucking throw me some dollars since I can't seem to get myself together to get them myself.

So I end up sitting at the table because, like Sister said, we are strong and I do need to eat the favorite meal from my childhood she's made for me. I need to be healthy so I can carry a child someday, to be a mama someday.

Sister asks the blessing. She thanks God for earlier today when she went to see Daddy and he saw her and was able to say "Baby girl." She asks God to protect Mama when she's closing at the liquor store in Rich Square. Mama works three part-time jobs to keep Daddy in that nice home. I'm trying to find a job, you know, but it's hard 'round here. And Sister asks God to be with me too. That's it. Just for God to be with me.

And the old fucker says "Amen" real loud like he'd been waiting for it to be over.

Jeopardy comes on and there's a whole column on the Black Plague. I am good at history.

And when My Man found out the old fucker liked history too, he said, "Look honey, here's something you can talk to him about. Here's a way to get to know him a little better. Do it for your sister."

I thought how wonderful and sweet and caring My Man was to say that and I say to the old fucker, "You wouldn't think it but I know a lot about the Black Plague."

The old fucker swallows the damn mouthful he has in and says, "Oh yeah, let's see who gets the most answers right."

And I don't want it to be a competition. I don't want it to go like that. So I say all I remember from the Black Plague was from where I was in the hospital and as high as I was on straight morphine injections in that port they ran through my arm straight to my heart, that documentary was the only thing I could understand. That when women found out they were sick, they would sew themselves up in their own death sacks made of cloth or burlap or whatever medieval thing was around so they wouldn't spread the disease to their loved ones. They'd tell their family, "As much as I fight to get out, don't let me."

And then I get up and say, "There is a charge for the eyeing of my scars, there is a charge for the beating of my heart, see it still goes and there is a charge." I'm pointing at my scars on my arms, standing at my sister's dinner table.

Sister just looks at her plate with big eyes.

The old fucker gets up from the table and says, "Some people just need to get their ass whooped."

I help my sister clean up. If that old fucker really loved my sister, he'd help her clean up. He'd help her get some tires riding to the next county, raining like it is. If he loved her, he'd give her that ring she wants. But he thinks our family is white trash and I think this because when our daddy was first in the nursing home and Mama didn't know how to deal and Sister came home and found her so drunk she was throwing up on herself in the bathtub, knowing that everyone around here knows our family needs prayers, that old fucker took advantage of my sister and put her reputation on the line and asked her to move in with him and his fourteen-year-old daughter when my Sister's twenty-four years younger than him and had never lived on her own. Also I had a nightmare one time that he made her pregnant and then he had to marry her.

I dry and put up the last plate and go and grab my wallet off the damn end table and sling the dollar bills I have at the old fucker on the recliner and say, "Here's some money for condoms."

"Some people just need a real good ass whoopin," he says to my sister in the kitchen. He's looking at the dollars on his gut.

The night me and My Man had sex on a Civil War battlefield we decided we'd name our daughter after it. It was a battlefield we'd never heard of, with the most pretty name. But I won't say that name. I don't want to jinx it. It's something only me and My Man know.

I've been writing about the future daughter we'd have. We always said she'd have my hair and his eyes. I've been writing about me and him raising her. Me sitting on the toilet watching him bathe her. Him telling her to hold her head back so the soap doesn't get in her eyes.

The first time I met My Man in real life, I had to find him in an antique store walking behind armoires and gun cabinets. He was the most beautiful thing I'd ever seen. Next time I saw him, I read him a poem I wrote for him. We were sitting in his truck, on top of a bridge, and I told him, "Let me be your shaman."

A few weeks after we broke up, I won't sad yet because I have been told that I compartmentalize things and he texted me referring to the shaman line. I texted back WHAT? I didn't remember what I had told him. And I'm ashamed of that.

I am standing in my sister's living room and *American Ninja Warrior* is on. No one can make it past the spider crawl. The old fucker has not picked the dollars off his gut.

I know it makes my sister upset that me and the man she loves don't get along. I told her at Sunday lunch I am trying to make peace with them being together but it's very uncomfortable for me. My mama was there and she overheard me and she said her and my sister could have been really rude to My Man after he gave me herpes but they didn't. "Something you'll have to live with for the rest of your life and might have effects on your children."

My sister is saying something to me from the kitchen. I think she's telling me to stay in. I'm not really paying attention to her because that hole in my mouth is hurting me. It almost always hurts after I eat. Food gets caught in it and I got to dig it out with my tongue or it'll get to tasting funny in my mouth. I haven't told Sister about that because that would be another thing she could hold against me. Another reason how I don't take care of myself. And if I can't take care of myself, I'll never be able to raise a family.

My keys are in my hand and I just run out the house. I drive to where all my family is buried. I ain't been out there in months.

It's still light out enough for me to see all the corn fields around the cemetery. I think more than any other crop, corn can really change a landscape 'cause it grows so tall. Look over it one day and you can see a house at the edge of the field, look another day and the house is gone. But this corn here looks strange. Just like tall stalks that ain't been cut down yet. They don't even have any ears on them. It's like they never growed. They never got enough rain during the summer. And I feel bad for that farmer.

I pull the weed and my piece out my glovebox. I got the piece because the color green reminded me of all those green glass vases Aunt Ginny had in her sunroom.

I get out the car and go see where Aunt Ginny is buried. The grass on top of her looks like golden brillo pad from where it ain't growed in with the other grass. But I know it will someday and she won't always be covered with a brillo pad carpet. And I ain't even high again yet.

I go sit where Grandaddy is buried. He's been dead five years now and don't have a headstone 'cause we can't afford it. That's also a bad feeling.

I take a hit and I feel it burn in my throat and when I exhale I feel like ghosts are coming out of me and I know that's lame and cliché right here at what might be called the emotional initial wound of the story. But almost everyone I know is already dead. Count them with me right here. There's Granddaddy and Grandma. There's Uncle Peachy and there's Aunt Ginny. There's Great Grandmama. And there's Mema. And then there's the ones I never knew in real life but they're walking in my head. There's Big Mama and Uncle Perry next to her. There's baby Stephen who died when he was three months old. There's Aunt Essie and her brother, my Great Grandaddy who was bow-legged.

At the old home place, I can look at pictures of them when they were young, and look out in the side yard and tell where they were standing. Long before they knew I'd ever be born. And I get Sister's fancy iPhone and take pictures of them and send them to my phone and I post them to Facebook. But no one knows them like me. They just look at my profile and think, "Oh there she is posting old black and white pics of her family again. I don't know them but I am going to like the pic anyway because maybe she knew them and maybe she misses them." And I am sad because no one is gonna know my family's stories because they were unimportant in the grand scheme of things. They made it through life without killing themselves and that is extraordinary enough for me.

Just like I don't know how Daddy didn't kill himself when he knew he was going to lose his mind and end up starving to death because he would forget how to swallow. Mama had to hide the guns in the house. And Daddy somehow was able to go to sleep at night.

Last time I saw him, his feet was swole with fluid from a urinary tract infection and he was barefoot 'cause he'd hid his shoes in another patient's room. His toenails were longer than I'd ever seen them in my life. His pants were falling off of him and he kept trying to take them off. The calendar in his room had not been turned over to the new month. He'd peed on the blanket on his bed. It smelled in the corner on the floor. The nurse came in and told me and Sister he'd taken a shit right in the middle of the dining room floor earlier in the week. And that he walked the halls at all hours of the night. He wouldn't lay down to sleep. We brought him candy. We had to show him how to eat it. He said three words. We couldn't make any of them out. I sat on his bed and looked out the window. I wanted to throw everything I could out of it. Including my body.

I look at pictures of Daddy when he was little on my phone before I go to sleep.

And in my dream world, I'd be leaning against his tombstone right now in this cemetery. I'd feel my backbone ridge into the letters that make up our last name. Then I'd push my shoulder blades out and push them into the stone as hard as I could.

I don't even know who is gonna pay for his tombstone when he dies either.

I hear some gunshots out back towards town. Folks stole the refrigerator out of the parsonage last week, when the Preacher was visiting the homebound. A girl from Ahoskie shot a man and his son over the weekend. Papers ain't said why yet. Mama says, "You've really got to love this place to stay."

And I take another hit, pull in deeper now. And I feel all my family out here under me and remember it ain't my life I'm living, it's theirs.

There was a time when I couldn't even get out of bed. I couldn't even eat or stand up straight. Mama put makeup on my face and when I opened my eyes those people at the end of my bed told me I was a miracle. I could smell all the flowers they brought me, rotting all around me in that tiny little room.

"There is a charge," the hole in my mouth says. That hit I just took then was real deeper. It's dark now and the smoke rises up to the moon. This is a good place now. My head doesn't feel like it's about to knock against the sky. That's a reference to a William Carlos Williams poem, about being so filled up with love you don't know what to do. I could recite it right now, *What have I to say to you when we shall meet? Yet—I lie here thinking of you.*

If I dug all the way down to Aunt Ginny right now, I could not make myself a baby again in her arms under the earth. I dream of myself as a baby in her coffin arms, in the nook between her ribs and little arm. The baby me in her dead arms. Curls in both our hair.

And Daddy won't be there to pick me up. If I get back home tonight, he won't be there reading an auto trader in the living room. And he won't be there in the morning to give me and Sister bowls of grits, to ask us if the little rats had a dance in our hair last night. To brush the tangles out.

And when we lost the house, me and Sister were cleaning out our bedrooms upstairs and there were so many doll babies we didn't want to save. "Don't you want to keep these for your little girls," Mama said. They told us if we left a mess in the house it didn't matter. The bank didn't care. Me and Sister threw our doll babies into the wall. Their heads busted open and we left them like that in the floor.

The last text I sent My Man was thirteen days ago, asking him if he still listened to that Roy Orbison tape I gave him. And how I listen to "In Dreams" now every night over and over because "In dreams I walk with you, in dreams I talk with you."

But in my dreams My Man looks at me like I'm a stranger. And like I said, I wake up crying.

Because even though when I asked My Man if he wanted me to disappear, he said no. He told me to do what I needed to do. Which was asking about that Roy Orbison tape. And I haven't heard from him and I know I may never hear from him again.

◊ ◊ ◊

The green's floating at the bottom of my sister's swimming pool like graceful moving jellyfish. I could drown there.

Or in the ocean. Daddy'd take us once a year. Throw us in and say, "This'll get the ticks and fleas off ya."

That's where I came up from the water and spat water in My Man's face for the first time. Then every shower. Except not the one I took earlier today. He won't there. I don't even remember now our last shower. We would wash each other's hair.

I want to be warm. I want to hold My Man's hand. I have to believe one day I'll be able to show My Man now the tops of the tombstones are silver little fingernails. A field full of half moons.

The last time we argued was about me going to the dentist. He said I needed to go. That he'd pay for it. I said I wouldn't 'cause as soon as I opened my mouth the dentist would say "You're a dumbass," and I'd say, "No I'm just poor." And I didn't want to have to say that.

I remember being in Christian camp and the Preacher made us feel like it was us who put Jesus on the cross. My sins of jealousy and not singing enough songs that praised the Lord. *In the sweet by and by we will meet at that beautiful shore.*

My body belongs to some creator. And I move because of it.

And I was taught every sin I committed was a strike into Jesus's back, ripping it open. We all watched that movie together in youth group, *The Passion of the Christ*, laying in the floor of the fellowship hall, for a sleepover. Jesus had to pull himself up with the nails in his wrists, not in the middle of the hands, which is traditionally what art says, and push himself up from that long nail in his ankle in order to take a breath because of the weight of gravity.

Paul wrote, "I rejoice in my suffering." And later, "For when I am weak, I am strong."

A hit. A hard one. I cough real bad. My stomach muscles cramp from where I was cut open like a hog. And I'm bending over, holding myself on the ground.

When I look up all the stars twinkle down on me.

My Man is fucking his girl in the truck, in the zoo parking lot and she doesn't know where to brace her feet to make it best but he doesn't care. Because he's not thinking about me right now.

I'd like to be hit even harder.

I bite my wrist as hard as I can and I get back in my car. I check my phone and I've got a bunch of missed calls from my sister. She says Daddy's home called. And Daddy was playing moving his cup all around his plate like he always does now, dropping bread in it. And another resident got upset about it and punched him twice in the face. Sister says Daddy didn't fight back. He won't even bruised but they had him on seventy-two hour watch during which they would check on him every thirty minutes. She is on the way to see him. I tell her I love her.

Driving now is floating just above the road and all around me is the flat, flat land. The tall shadows of the woods cut between the fields and sky. I really like the feeling when you're choking and he holds you down longer than the time before. More and more closer every time to a place I don't know.

I want to see Daddy's chopping block. So I drive to that house on Chestnut Street. I will go up and ring the doorbell. If no one comes, I will punch the window next to me and see if I can unlock the door. If no alarm goes off, I will make my way inside.

No lights are on in the house. The chopping block is in the middle of the kitchen floor just like old times. The knives are next to the stove and the one I want to use is good and sharp. I spin the tip into the end of my finger like the movies.

The fridge's got an untouched, brand new rotisserie chicken. I'm another person in another time with my same blood running through me, standing on the back steps, looking at my great grandma in the backyard holding the chicken above her head, breaking its neck with the flick of her wrist.

I grab the chicken where its neck ends and put it on the chopping block. I stab it, rip it in two. Down into the bottom of the valley in the chopping block. Where Daddy showed me the wood wore down when I was little. Where the butchers cut the meat up the most.

I know both how to be abased, and I know how to abound; everywhere and in all things I am instructed both to be full and to be hungry, both to abound and to suffer need.

I'm being still now, to listen. To see if God will have anything to say.

◊ ◊ ◊

I hear the steps of a little child coming to me. One I can tuck
into bed by reading a book.

Before she goes to sleep tonight, my sister's saying a special
prayer for that little one year old boy down the road who shot
himself in the heart with a staple gun.

But the sound is not from a child, it's a light coming on and
that couple coming on either side of me. They're telling my
name to me and they're telling me it's okay. "Calm down, now,"
they're saying with calm faces.

The chicken meat sticks to me like slugs. I want to go home
and cry in my bed. I want to cry until I am empty.

They have taken away the knife and are on either side of me,
leading me out the house. They have soft hands. The woman is
stroking my arm. The man gets in a car and the woman stands
in front of me. She holds both my shoulders. She says, "Let's get
you home." She pulls meat out of my hair.

They turn the heat on in the car and it feels so nice. I remember to tell them I'll fix their window. I don't know how, but I'll
do it.

And they say "Okay."

They don't ask me where I live. Everybody already knows.

Notes

Several of the stories first appeared, in slightly different form, in the following publications:

"An Unspoken" in *The Paris Review*
"The Virgin" in *The Oxford American*
"Charlie Elliott" in *3:AM Magazine*
"The Locket" as "Norma" in *Joyland*
"Snowball Jr." in *New York Tyrant*
"Uncle Elmer" in *Juked*
"Lorene" in *People Holding*
"Sister" as "June Bugs" in *Empty House Press*
"Shania" in *The Nervous Breakdown*
"Sleepovers" in *Hobart*
"The Chopping Block" as "In Dreams" in *Vote No On Amendment 1 E-Zine*
"Return to the Coondog Castle" in *Parhelion Literary Magazine*
"Mind Craft" as "Mine Craft" in *SHOW YOUR SKIN*
"The Bass" in *Bull*
"The Truth About Miss Katie" in *Tusk*

— C. MICHAEL CURTIS —
SHORT STORY BOOK PRIZE

The C. MICHAEL CURTIS SHORT STORY BOOK PRIZE includes $10,000 and book publication. The prize is named in honor of C. Michael Curtis, who has served as an editor of The Atlantic since 1963 and as fiction editor since 1982. This prize is made possible by an anonymous contribution from a South Carolina donor. The namesake of the prize, C. Michael Curtis, has discovered or edited some of the finest short story writers of the modern era, including Tobias Wolff, Joyce Carol Oates, John Updike, and Anne Beattie.

RECENT WINNERS

Let Me Out Here • Emily W. Pease

PUBLISHING
New & Extraordinary
VOICES FROM THE
AMERICAN SOUTH

HUB CITY PRESS has emerged as the South's premier independent literary press. Focused on finding and spotlighting new and extraordinary voices from the American South, the press has published over eighty high-caliber literary works. Hub City is interested in books with a strong sense of place and is committed to introducing a diverse roster of lesser-heard Southern voices. We are funded by the National Endowment for the Arts, the South Carolina Arts Commission and hundreds of donors across the Carolinas.

RECENT HUB CITY PRESS FICTION

The Prettiest Star • Carter Sickels

Watershed • Mark Barr

A Wild Eden • Scott Sharpe

The Magnetic Girl • Jessica Handler

What Luck, This Life • Kathryn Schwille

Sabon MT Pro
10.8/15.3